MIDNIGHT IN DEATH
AND INTERLUDE IN DEATH

In *Midnight in Death*, Eve Dallas's name has made a Christmas list, but it's not for being naughty or nice — it's for putting a serial killer behind bars. Now he's escaped and has her in his sights . . . While in *Interlude in Death*, when respected Commander Skinner offers her a promotion if she'll give her husband Roarke up to custody, her reaction is furious. Roarke's Irish past is murky, but he's a changed man — so what is the commander after? With Eve and Skinner at one of Roarke's holiday resorts for a police convention, Skinner's thwarted vengeance soon brings death to their luxury surroundings.

SPECIAL MESSAGE TO READERS

THE ULVERSCROFT FOUNDATION
(registered UK charity number 264873)
was established in 1972 to provide funds for
research, diagnosis and treatment of eye diseases.
Examples of major projects funded by
the Ulverscroft Foundation are:-

- The Children's Eye Unit at Moorfields Eye Hospital, London
- The Ulverscroft Children's Eye Unit at Great Ormond Street Hospital for Sick Children
- Funding research into eye diseases and treatment at the Department of Ophthalmology, University of Leicester
- The Ulverscroft Vision Research Group, Institute of Child Health
- Twin operating theatres at the Western Ophthalmic Hospital, London
- The Chair of Ophthalmology at the Royal Australian College of Ophthalmologists

You can help further the work of the Foundation
by making a donation or leaving a legacy.
Every contribution is gratefully received. If you
would like to help support the Foundation or
require further information, please contact:

**THE ULVERSCROFT FOUNDATION
The Green, Bradgate Road, Anstey
Leicester LE7 7FU, England
Tel: (0116) 236 4325**

website: www.foundation.ulverscroft.com

MIDNIGHT IN DEATH AND INTERLUDE IN DEATH

J. D. ROBB

ISIS
LARGE
PRINT

First published in Great Britain 2013
by
Piatkus
an imprint of Little, Brown Book Group

First Isis Edition
published 2016
by arrangement with
Little, Brown Book Group
An Hachette UK Company

The moral right of the author has been asserted

All characters and events in this publication, other than
those clearly in the public domain, are fictitious and any
resemblance to real persons, living or dead, is purely
coincidental.

Copyright © 2012 by Nora Roberts
All rights reserved

A catalogue record for this book is available
from the British Library.

ISBN 978–1–78541–147–2 (hb)
ISBN 978–1–78541–153–3 (pb)

Published by
F. A. Thorpe (Publishing)
Anstey, Leicestershire

Set by Words & Graphics Ltd.
Anstey, Leicestershire
Printed and bound in Great Britain by
T. J. International Ltd., Padstow, Cornwall

This book is printed on acid-free paper

MIDNIGHT
IN DEATH

STAFFORDSHIRE
LIBRARIES, ARTS
AND ARCHIVES

045685069

ULVERSCROFT 2 1 JAN 2016

F   £20·95

The year is dying in the night.
ALFRED, LORD TENNYSON

The welfare of the people is the chief law.
CICERO

CHAPTER
ONE

Murder respects no traditions. It ignores sentiment. It takes no holidays.

Because murder was her business, Lieutenant Eve Dallas stood in the predawn freeze of Christmas morning coating the deerskin gloves her husband had given her only hours before with Seal-It.

The call had come in less than an hour before and less than six hours since she'd closed a case that had left her shaky and exhausted. Her first Christmas with Roarke wasn't getting off to a rousing start.

Then again, it had taken a much nastier turn for Judge Harold Wainger.

His body had been dumped dead center in the ice rink at Rockefeller Center. Face up, so his glazed eyes could stare at the huge celebrational tree that was New York's symbol of goodwill toward men.

His body was naked and already a deep shade of blue. The thick mane of silver hair that had been his trademark had been roughly chopped off. And though his face was severely battered, Eve had no trouble recognizing him.

She'd sat in his courtroom dozens of times in her ten years on the force. He had been, she thought, a solid and steady man, with as much understanding of the slippery channels of the law as respect for the heart of it.

She crouched down to get a closer look at the words that had been burned deeply into his chest.

JUDGE NOT, LEST YOU BE JUDGED

She hoped the burns had been inflicted postmortem, but she doubted it.

He had been mercilessly beaten, the fingers of both hands broken. Deep wounds around his wrists and ankles indicated that he'd been bound. But it hadn't been the beating or the burns that killed him.

The rope used to hang him was still around his neck, digging deep into flesh. Even that wouldn't have been quick, she decided. It didn't appear that his neck had been broken, and the burst vessels in his eyes and face signaled slow strangulation.

"He wanted you alive as long as possible," she murmured.

"He wanted you to feel it all."

Kneeling now, she studied the handwritten note that was flapping gaily in the wind. It had been fixed over the judge's groin like an obscene loincloth. The list of names had been printed in careful square block letters.

JUDGE HAROLD WAINGER
PROSECUTING ATTORNEY STEPHANIE RING
PUBLIC DEFENDER CARL NEISSAN
JUSTINE POLINSKY

DOCTOR CHARLOTTE MIRA
LIEUTENANT EVE DALLAS

"Saving me for last, Dave?"

She recognized the style: gleeful infliction of pain followed by a slow, torturous death. David Palmer enjoyed his work. His experiments, as he'd called them when Eve had finally hunted him down three years before.

By the time she'd gotten him into a cage, he had eight victims to his credit, and with them an extensive file of discs recording his work. Since then he'd been serving the eight life-term sentences that Wainger had given him in a maximum-security ward for mental defectives.

"But you got out, didn't you, Dave? This is your handiwork. The torture, the humiliations, the burns. Public dumping spot for the body. No copycat here. Bag him," she ordered and got wearily to her feet.

It didn't look as though the last days of December 2058 were going to be much of a party.

The minute she was back in her vehicle, Eve ordered the heat on full blast. She stripped off her gloves and rubbed her hands over her face. She would have to go in and file her report, but the first order of business couldn't wait for her to drive to her home office. Damn if she was going to spend Christmas Day at Cop Central.

She used the in-dash 'link to contact Dispatch and arrange to have each name on the list notified of possible jeopardy. Christmas or not, she was ordering uniformed guards on each one.

As she drove, she engaged her computer. "Computer, status on David Palmer, mental-defective inmate on Rexal penal facility."

Working . . . David Palmer, sentenced to eight consecutive life terms in off-planet facility Rexal, reported escaped during transport to prison infirmary, December nineteen. Man-hunt ongoing.

"I guess Dave decided to come home for the holidays." She glanced up, scowling, as a blimp cruised over, blasting Christmas tunes as dawn broke over the city. Screw the herald angels, she thought, and called her commander.

"Sir," she said when Whitney's face filled her screen. "I'm sorry to disturb your Christmas."

"I've already been notified about Judge Wainger. He was a good man."

"Yes, sir, he was." She noted that Whitney was wearing a robe — a thick, rich burgundy that she imagined had been a gift from his wife. Roarke was always giving her fancy presents. She wondered if Whitney was as baffled by them as she usually was. "His body's being transferred to the morgue. I have the evidence sealed and am en route to my home office now."

"I would have preferred another primary on this, Lieutenant." He saw her tired eyes flash, the golden brown darkening. Still, her face, with its sharp angles, the firm chin with its shallow dent, the full, unsmiling mouth, stayed cool and controlled.

"Do you intend to remove me from the case?"

"You've just come off a difficult and demanding investigation. Your aide was attacked."

"I'm not calling Peabody in," Eve said quickly. "She's had enough."

"And you haven't?"

She opened her mouth, closed it again. Tricky ground, she acknowledged. "Commander, my name's on the list."

"Exactly. One more reason for you to take a pass here."

Part of her wanted to — the part that wanted, badly, to put it all aside for the day, to go home and have the kind of normal Christmas she'd never experienced. But she thought of Wainger, stripped of all life and all dignity.

"I tracked David Palmer, and I broke him. He was my collar, and no one knows the inside of his mind the way I do."

"Palmer?" Whitney's wide brow furrowed. "Palmer's in prison."

"Not any more. He escaped on the nineteenth. And he's back, Commander. You could say I recognized his signature. The names on the list," she continued, pressing her point. "They're all connected to him. Wainger was the judge during his trial. Stephanie Ring was APA. Cicely Towers prosecuted the case, but she's dead. Ring assisted. Carl Neissan was his court-appointed attorney when Palmer refused to hire his own counsel, Justine Polinksy served as jury foreman. Dr Mira tested him and testified against him at trial. I brought him in."

"The names on the list need to be notified."

"Already done, sir, and bodyguards assigned. I can pull the data from the files into my home unit to refresh my memory, but it's fairly fresh as it is. You don't forget someone like David Palmer. Another primary will have to start at the beginning, taking time that we don't have. I know this man, how he works, how he thinks. What he wants."

"What he wants, Lieutenant?"

"What he always wanted. Acknowledgment for his genius."

"It's your case, Dallas," Whitney said after a long silence. "Close it."

"Yes, sir."

She broke transmission as she drove through the gates of the staggering estate that Roarke had made his home.

Ice from the previous night's storm glinted like silver silk on naked branches. Ornamental shrubs and evergreens glistened with it. Beyond them, the house rose and spread, an elegant fortress, a testament to an earlier century with its beautiful stone, its acres of glass.

In the gloomy half-light of morning, gorgeously decorated trees shimmered in several windows. Roarke, she thought with a little smile, had gotten heavily into the Christmas spirit.

Neither of them had had much in the way of pretty holiday trees with gaily wrapped gifts stacked under them in their lives. Their childhoods had been miseries, and they had compensated for it in different ways. His had been to acquire, to become one of the richest and most powerful men in the world. By whatever means available. Hers had been to take control, to become part of the system that had failed her when she was a child.

Hers was law. His was — or had been — circumventing law.

Now, not quite a year since another murder had put them on the same ground, they were a unit. She wondered if she would ever understand how they'd managed it.

She left her car out front, walked up the steps and through the door into the kind of wealth that fantasies were made of. Old polished wood, sparkling crystal, ancient rugs lovingly preserved, art that museums would have wept for.

She shrugged off her jacket, started to toss it over the newel post. Then, gritting her teeth, she backtracked and hung it up. She and Summerset, Roarke's aide-de-camp, had declared a tacit truce in their sniping war. There would be no potshots on Christmas, she decided.

She could stand it if he could.

Only marginally pleased that he didn't slither into the foyer and hiss at her as he normally did, Eve headed into the main parlor.

Roarke was there, sitting by the fire, reading the first-edition copy of Yeats that she'd given him. It had been the only gift she'd been able to come up with for the man who not only had everything but owned most of the plants where it was manufactured.

He glanced up, smiled at her. Her stomach fluttered, as it so often did. Just a look, just a smile, and her system went jittery. He looked so . . . perfect, she thought. He was dressed casually for the day, in black, his long, lean body relaxing in a chair probably made two hundred years before.

He had the face of a god with slightly wicked intentions, eyes of blazing Irish blue and a mouth created to destroy a woman's control. Power sat attractively on him, as sleek and sexy, Eve thought, as the rich fall of black hair that skimmed nearly to his shoulders.

He closed the book, set it aside, then held out a hand to her.

"I'm sorry I had to leave." She crossed to him, linked her fingers with his. "I'm sorrier that I'm going to have to go up and work, at least for a few hours."

"Got a minute first?"

"Yeah, maybe. Just." And she let him pull her down into his lap. Let herself close her eyes and simply wallow there, in the scent and the feel of him. "Not exactly the kind of day you'd planned."

"That's what I get for marrying a cop." Ireland sang quietly in his voice, the lilt of a sexy poet. "For loving one," he added, and tipped her face up to kiss her.

"It's a pretty lousy deal right now."

"Not from where I'm sitting." He combed his fingers through her short brown hair. "You're what I want, Eve, the woman who leaves her home to stand over the dead. And the one who knew what a copy of Yeats would mean to me."

"I'm better with the dead than with buying presents. Otherwise I'd have come up with more than one."

She looked over at the small mountain of gifts under the tree — gifts it had taken her more than an hour to open. And her wince made him laugh.

"You know, one of the greatest rewards in giving you presents, Lieutenant, is the baffled embarrassment they cause you."

"I hope you got it out of your system for a while."

"Mmm," was his only response. She wasn't used to gifts, he thought, hadn't been given anything as a child but pain. "Have you decided what to do with the last one?"

The final box he'd given her had been empty, and he'd enjoyed seeing her frown in puzzlement. Just as he'd enjoyed seeing her grin at him when he told her it was a day. A day she could fill with whatever she liked. He would take her wherever she wanted to go, and they would do whatever she wanted to do. Off-planet or on. In reality or through the holo-room.

Any time, any place, any world was hers for the asking.

"No, I haven't had much time to think it through. It's a pretty great gift. I don't want to screw it up."

She let herself relax against him another moment with the fire crackling, the tree shimmering, then she pulled back. "I've got to get started. There's a lot of drone work on this one, and I don't want to tag Peabody today."

"Why don't I give you a hand?" He smiled again at the automatic refusal he read in her eyes. "Step into Peabody's sturdy shoes for the day."

"This one's not connected to you in any way. I want to keep it that way."

"All the better." He nudged her up, got to his feet. "I can help you do the runs or whatever, and that way you won't have to spend your entire Christmas chained to your desk."

She started to refuse again, then reconsidered. Most of the data she wanted were public domain in any case. And what wasn't was nothing she wouldn't have shared with him if she'd been thinking it through aloud.

Besides, he was good.

"Okay, consider yourself a drone. But when Peabody's got her balance, you're out."

"Darling." He took her hand, kissed it, watched her scowl. "Since you ask so sweetly."

"And no sloppy stuff," she put in. "I'm on duty."

CHAPTER
TWO

The huge cat, Galahad, was draped over the back of Eve's sleep chair like a drunk over a bar at last call. Since he'd spent several hours the night before attacking boxes, fighting with ribbon, and murdering discarded wrapping paper, she left him where he was so he could sleep it off.

Eve set down her bag and went directly to the AutoChef for coffee. "The guy we're after is David Palmer."

"You've already identified the killer."

"Oh, yeah, I know who I'm after. Me and Dave, we're old pals."

Roarke took the mug she brought him, watched her through the steam. "The name's vaguely familiar to me."

"You'd have heard it. It was all over the media three, three and a half years ago. I need all my case files on that investigation, all data on the trial. You can start by —" She broke off when he laid a hand on her arm.

"David Palmer — serial killer. Torture murders." It was playing back for him, in bits and pieces. "Fairly young. What — mid-twenties?"

"Twenty-two at time of arrest. A real prodigy, our Dave. He considers himself a scientist, a visionary. His

15

mission is to explore and record the human mind's tolerance to extreme duress — pain, fear, starvation, dehydration, sensory deprivation. He could talk a good game, too." She sipped her coffee. "He'd sit there in interview, his pretty face all lit with enthusiasm, and explain that once we knew the mind's breaking point, we'd be able to enhance it, to strengthen it. He figured since I was a cop, I'd be particularly interested in his work. Cops are under a great deal of stress, often finding ourselves in life-and-death situations where the mind is easily distracted by fear or outside stimuli. The results of his work could be applied to members of the police and security forces, the military, even in business situations."

"I didn't realize he was yours."

"Yeah, he was mine." She shrugged her shoulders. "I was a little more low profile in those days."

He might have smiled at that, knowing it was partially her connection to him that had changed that status. But he remembered too much of the Palmer case to find the humor. "I was under the impression that he was safely locked away."

"Not safely enough. He slipped out. The victim this morning was dumped in a public area — another of Dave's trademarks. He likes us to know he's hard at work. The autopsy will have to verify, but the victim was tortured pre-mortem. I'd guess Dave found himself a new hole to work in and had the judge there at least a day before killing him. Death by strangulation occurred on or around midnight. Merry Christmas, Judge Wainger," she murmured.

"And that would be the judge who tried his case."

"Yeah." Absently, she put her mug down, reached into her bag for a copy of the sealed note she'd already sent to the lab. "He left a calling card — another signature. All these names are connected to his case and his sentencing. Part of his work this time around would be, at my guess, letting his intended victims stew about what he has in store for them. They're being contacted and protected. He'll have a tough time getting to any of them."

"And you?" Roarke spoke with studied calm after a glance at the list, and his wife's name. "Where's your protection?"

"I'm a cop. I'm the one who does the protecting."

"He'll want you most, Eve."

She turned. However controlled his voice was, she heard the anger under it. "Maybe, but not as much as I want him."

"You stopped him," Roarke continued. "Whatever was done after — the tests, the trial, the sentence — was all a result of your work. You'll matter most."

"Let's leave those conclusions to the profiler." Though she agreed with them. "I'm going to contact Mira as soon as I look through the case files again. You can access those for me while I start my prelim report. I'll give you the codes for my office unit and the Palmer files."

Now he lifted a brow, smiled smugly. "Please. I can't work if you insult me."

"Sorry." She picked up her coffee again. "I don't know why I pretend you need codes to access any damn thing."

"Neither do I."

He sat down to retrieve the data she wanted, moving smoothly through the task. It was pitifully simple for him, and his mind was left free to consider. To decide.

She'd said he wasn't connected to this, and that she expected him to back away when Peabody was on duty again. But she was wrong. Her name on the list meant he was more involved than he'd ever been before. And no power on earth, not even that of the woman he loved, would cause him to back away.

Close by, Eve worked on the auxiliary unit, recording the stark facts into the report. She wanted the autopsy results, the crime scene team and sweeper data. But she had little hope that she would get anything from the spotty holiday staff before the end of the next day.

Struggling not to let her irritation with Christmas resurface, she answered her beeping 'link. "Dallas."

"Lieutenant, Officer Miller here."

"What is it, Miller?"

"Sir, my partner and I were assigned to contact and guard APA Ring. We arrived at her residence shortly after seven-thirty. There was no response to our knock."

"This is a priority situation, Miller. You're authorized to enter the premises."

"Yes, sir. Understood. We did so. The subject is not in residence. My partner questioned the across-the-hall neighbor. The subject left early yesterday morning to spend the holiday with her family in Philadelphia. Lieutenant, she never arrived. Her father reported her missing this morning."

18

Eve's stomach tightened. Too late, she thought. Already too late. "What was her method of transpo, Miller?"

"She had her own car. We're en route to the garage where she stored it."

"Keep me posted, Miller." Eve broke transmission, looked over, and met Roarke's eyes. "He's got her. I'd like to think she ran into some road hazard or hired a licensed companion for a quick holiday fling before heading on to her family, but he's got her. I need the 'link codes for the other names on the list."

"You'll have them. One minute."

She didn't need the code for one of the names. With her heart beating painfully, she put the call through to Mira's home. A small boy answered with a grin and a giggle. "Merry Christmas! This is Grandmom's house."

For a moment Eve just blinked, wondering how she'd gotten the wrong code. Then she heard the familiar soft voice in the background, saw Mira come on screen with a smile on her face and strain in her eyes.

"Eve. Good morning. Would you hold for a moment, please? I'd like to take this upstairs. No, sweetie," she said to the boy who tugged on her sleeve. "Run play with your new toys. I'll be back. Just a moment, Eve."

The screen went to a calm, cool blue, and Eve exhaled gratefully. Relief at finding Mira home, alive, well, safe — and the oddity of thinking of the composed psychiatrist as Grandmom played through her mind.

"I'm sorry." Mira came back on. "I didn't want to take this downstairs with my family."

"No problem. Are the uniforms there?"

19

"Yes." In a rare show of nerves, Mira pushed a hand through her sable-toned hair. "Miserable duty for them, sitting out in a car on Christmas. I haven't figured out how to have them inside and keep my family from knowing. My children are here, Eve, my grandchildren. I need to know if you believe there's any chance they're in danger."

"No." She said it quick and firm. "That's not his style. Dr Mira, you're not to leave the house without your guards. You're to go nowhere, not the office, not the corner deli, without both of them. Tomorrow you'll be fitted for a tracer bracelet."

"I'll take all the precautions, Eve."

"Good, because one of those precautions is to cancel all patient appointments until Palmer is in custody."

"That's ridiculous."

"You're to be alone with no one, at any time. So unless your patients agree to let you walk around in their heads while a couple of cops are looking on, you're taking a vacation."

Mira eyed Eve steadily. "And are you about to take a vacation?"

"I'm about to do my job. Part of that job is you. Stephanie Ring is missing." She waited, one beat only, for the implication to register. "Do what you're told, Dr Mira, or you'll be in protective custody within the hour. I'll need a consult tomorrow, nine o'clock. I'll come to you."

She broke transmission, turned to get the 'link codes from Roarke, and found him watching her steadily. "What?"

"She means a great deal to you. If she meant less, you'd have handled that with more finesse."

"I don't have much finesse at the best of times. Let's have the codes." When he hesitated, she sighed and replied, "Okay, okay, fine. She means a lot, and I'll be damned if he'll get within a mile of her. Now give me the goddamn codes."

"Already transferred to your unit, Lieutenant. Logged in, on memory. You've only to state the name of the party for transmission."

"Show-off." She muttered it, knowing it would make him grin, and turned back to contact the rest of the names on Palmer's list.

When she was satisfied that the other targets were where they were supposed to be, and under guard, Eve turned to the case files Roarke had accessed.

She spent an hour going over data and reports, another reviewing her interview discs with Palmer.

Okay, Dave, tell me about Michelle Hammel. What made her special?

David Palmer, a well-built man of twenty-two with the golden good looks of the wealthy New England family he'd sprung from, smiled and leaned forward earnestly. His clear blue eyes were bright with enthusiasm. His caramel-cream complexion glowed with health and vitality.

Somebody's finally listening, Eve remembered thinking as she saw herself as she'd been three years before. He's finally got the chance to share his genius.

Her hair was badly cut — she'd still been hacking at it herself in those days. The boots crossed at her ankles had been new then and almost unscarred. There was no wedding ring on her finger.

Otherwise, she thought, she was the same.

She was young, fit. An athlete, Palmer told her. Very disciplined, mind and body. A long-distance runner — Olympic hopeful. She knew how to block pain, how to focus on a goal. She'd be at the top end of the scale, you see. Just as Leroy Greene was at the bottom. He'd fogged his mind with illegals for years. No tolerance for disruptive stimuli. He lost all control even before the application of pain. His mind broke as soon as he regained consciousness and found himself strapped to the table. But Michelle . . .

She fought? She held out?

Palmer nodded cheerfully. She was magnificent, really. She struggled against the restraints, then stopped when she understood that she wouldn't be able to free herself. There was fear. The monitors registered her rise in pulse rate, blood pressure, all vital physical and emotional signs. I have excellent equipment.

Yeah, I've seen it. Top of the line.

It's vital work. His eyes had clouded then, unfocused as they did when he spoke of the import of his experiments. You'll see if you review the data on Michelle that she centered her fear, used it to keep herself alive. She controlled it, initially, tried to reason with me. She made promises, she pretended to understand my research, even to help me. She was clever. When she understood that wouldn't help her, she cursed me, pumping up her adrenaline as I introduced new pain stimuli.

"He broke her feet," Eve said, knowing Roarke was watching behind her. "Then her arms. He was right about his equipment back then. He had electrodes that when attached to different parts of the body, or placed in various orifices, administered graduating levels of electric shock. He kept Michelle alive for three days until the torture broke her. She was begging for him to kill her toward the end. He used a rope and pulley system to hang her — gradual strangulation. She was nineteen."

Roarke laid his hands on her shoulders. "You stopped him once, Eve, you'll stop him again."

"Damn right I will."

She looked up when she heard someone coming quickly down the corridor. "Save data, and file," she ordered just as Nadine Furst came into the room. Perfect, she thought, a visit from one of Channel 75's top on-air reporters. The fact that they were friends didn't make Eve any less wary.

"Out paying Christmas calls, Nadine?"

"I got a present this morning." Nadine tossed a disc on the desk.

Eve looked at it, then back up at Nadine's face. It was pale, the sharp features drawn. For once, Nadine wasn't perfectly groomed with lip dye, enhancers, and every hair in place. She looked more than frazzled, Eve realized. She looked afraid.

"What's the problem?"

"David Palmer."

Slowly Eve got to her feet. "What about him?"

"Apparently he knows what I do for a living, and that we're friendly. He sent me that." She glanced back down at the disc, struggled to suppress a shudder.

23

"Hoping I'd do a feature story on him — and his work — and share the contents of his disc with you. Can I have a drink? Something strong."

Roarke came around the desk and eased her into a chair. "Sit down. You're cold," he murmured when he took her hands.

"Yeah, I am. I've been cold ever since I ran that disc."

"I'll get you a brandy."

Nadine nodded in agreement, then fisted her hands in her lap and looked at Eve. "There are two other people on the recording. One of them is Judge Wainger. What's left of Judge Wainger. And there's a woman, but I can't recognize her. She's — he's already started on her."

"Here." Roarke brought the snifter, gently wrapped Nadine's hands around the bowl. "Drink this."

"Okay." She lifted the glass, took one long sip, and felt the blast of heat explode in her gut. "Dallas, I've seen a lot of bad things. I've reported them, I've studied them. But I've never seen anything like this. I don't know how you deal with it, day after day."

"One day at a time." Eve picked up the disc. "You don't have to watch this again."

"Yes." Nadine drank again, let out a long breath. "I do."

Eve turned the disc over in her hand. It was a standard-use model. They'd never trace it. She slid it into her unit. "Copy disc and run, display on screen."

David Palmer's youthful and handsome face swam onto the wall screen.

"Ms Furst, or may I call you Nadine? So much more personal that way, and my work is very personal to me. I've admired your work, by the way. It's one of the reasons I'm trusting you to get my story on air. You believe in what you do, don't you, Nadine?"

His eyes were serious now, professional to professional, his face holding all the youth and innocence of a novitiate at the altar. "Those of us who reach for perfection believe in what we do," he continued. "I'm aware that you have a friendly relationship with Lieutenant Dallas. The lieutenant and I also have a relationship, perhaps not so friendly, but we do connect, and I do admire her stamina. I hope you'll share the contents of this disc with her as soon as possible. By this time she should already be heading the investigation into the death of Judge Wainger."

His smile went bright now, and just a little mad at the edges. "Hello, Lieutenant. You'll excuse me if I just conclude my business with Nadine. I want Dallas to be closely involved. It's important to me. You will tell my story, won't you, Nadine? Let the public themselves judge, not some narrow-minded fool in a black robe."

The next scene slipped seamlessly into place, the audio high so that the woman's screams seemed to rip the air in the room where Eve sat, watching.

Judge Wainger's body was bound hand and foot and suspended several inches from a plain concrete floor. A basic pulley system this time, Eve mused. He'd taken time to set up some of the niceties, but it wasn't yet the complex, and yes, ingenious, system of torture that he'd created before.

Still, it worked very well.

Wainger's face was livid with agony, the muscles twitching as Palmer burned letters in his chest with a hand laser. He only moaned, his head lolling. Nearby, a system of monitors beeped and buzzed.

"He's failing, you see," Palmer said briskly in a voice-over. "His mind is moving beyond the pain, as it can no longer endure it. His system will attempt to shut down into unconsciousness. That can be reversed, as you'll see here." On screen, he flipped a switch. There was a high whine, then Wainger's body jerked. This time he screamed.

Across the room a woman shrieked and sobbed. The cage she was in swung wildly on its cable and was only big enough to allow her to crouch on hands and knees. A dark fall of hair covered most of her face, but Eve knew her.

Stephanie Ring was Palmer's.

When he turned, engaged another control, the cage sparked and shook. The woman let out a piercing wail, shuddered convulsively, then collapsed.

Palmer turned to the camera, smiled. "She's distracting, but I have only so much time. It's necessary to begin one subject before completing work on another. But her turn will come shortly. Subject Wainger's heart is failing. The data on him are nearly complete."

Using the ropes, he manually lowered Wainger to the floor. Eve noted the flex and bunch of muscles in Palmer's arms. "Dave's been pumping," she murmured.

"Getting in shape. He knew he'd have to work harder this round. He likes to prepare."

Palmer slipped a perfectly knotted noose around Wainger's neck and meticulously slid the trailing end through a metal ring in the ceiling. Leading it down, he threaded it through another ring in the floor, then pulled out the slack until Wainger rose to his knees, then his feet, and began gasping for air.

"Stop it, will you?" Nadine leapt to her feet. "I can't watch this again. I thought I could. I can't."

"Stop disc." Eve waited until the screen went blank, then went over to crouch in front of Nadine. "I'm sorry."

"No. I'm sorry. I thought I was tough."

"You are. Nobody's this tough."

Nadine shook her head and, finishing her brandy with one deep gulp, set the snifter aside. "You are. You don't let it get to you."

"It gets to me. But this is for me. I'm going to have a couple of uniforms come and take you home. They're going to hang with you everywhere until Palmer's down."

"You think he'll come after me?"

"No, but why take chances? Go home, Nadine. Put it away."

But after she'd asked Roarke to take Nadine downstairs to wait for the escort, Eve finished watching the disc. And at the end her eyes met Palmer's as he moved toward the camera.

"Subject Wainger died at midnight, December twenty-fourth. You'll last longer, Dallas. We both know that. You'll be my most fascinating subject. I have such wonders planned for you. You'll find me. I know you will. I'm counting on it. Happy holidays."

CHAPTER
THREE

Stephanie Ring's car was still in its permit slot in the garage. Her luggage was neatly stowed in the trunk. Eve circled the vehicle, searching for any sign of struggle, any evidence that might have been dropped and gone unnoticed during the snatch.

"He's got two basic MOs," she said, as much to herself as to the uniforms waiting nearby. "One is to gain entrance into the victims' homes by a ruse — delivery, repair, or service con; the other is to come on them in an unpopulated area. He spends time getting to know their routines and habits, the usual routes and schedules. He keeps all that in a log — very organized, scientific, along with bio data on each of them."

They weren't lab rats to him, she mused. It was personal, individualized. That was what excited him.

"In either case," she went on, "he uses a stunner, takes them down quickly, then transports them in his own vehicle. Security cameras operational in here?"

"Yes, sir." One of the uniforms passed her a sealed package of discs. "We confiscated them for the last three days, assuming that the subject may have stalked the victim previous to her abduction."

Eve lifted a brow. "Miller, right?"

"Sir."

"Good thinking. There's nothing more you can do here. Go home and eat some goose."

They didn't exactly race away, but neither did they linger. Eve put the package in her bag and turned to Roarke. "Why don't you do the same, pal? I'll only be a couple of hours."

"We'll only be a couple of hours."

"I don't need an aide to do a pass through Ring's apartment."

Roarke simply took her arm and led her back to the car. "You let the two uniforms go," he began as he started the engine. "Everyone else on Palmer's list is under guard. Why aren't you?"

"We covered that already."

"Partially." He reversed and headed out of the garage. "But I know you, Lieutenant. You're hoping he'll shuffle the order and come after you next. And you don't want some big-shouldered uniforms scaring him off."

For a moment she just drummed her fingers on her knee. In less than a year, the man had learned her inside and out. She wasn't entirely comfortable with that. "And your point would be?"

He nearly smiled at the annoyance in her voice. "I admire my wife's courage, her dedication to duty."

"You tossed in 'my wife' to irritate me, didn't you?"

"Of course." Satisfied, he picked up her hand, kissed the knuckles. "I'm sticking, Eve. Deal with it."

The pass through Stephanie Ring's apartment was no more than routine, and it turned up nothing but the tidy life of a single career woman who enjoyed surrounding herself with attractive things, spending her city salary on a stylish wardrobe.

Eve thought of the naked woman crouched like an animal in a cage, screaming in terror.

He's killing her now. Eve knew it. And she had no power to stop him.

When she was back in her home office, she reviewed the disc Palmer had sent Nadine. This time she willed herself to ignore what was happening and focus only on the surroundings.

"No windows," she commented. "The floor and walls look like concrete and old brick. The whole area can't be over thirty feet by twenty. It's probably a basement. Computer, pause. Enhance sector eight through fifteen. Magnify."

She paced as the computer went to work, then moved closer to the screen. "There, that's a stair tread. Steps, part of a railing. Behind it is some sort of — what is it — old furnace unit or water tank. He's found himself a hole. It has to be private," she continued, studying the view. "He can't do his work in a building where people might hear. Even if it's soundproofed, he'd risk someone poking around. Maintenance crew, repair team. Anything like that."

"Not an apartment or office building," Roarke agreed. "And with the steps it's not likely a storage facility. From the look of the furnace, it's a good-sized building, but far from new. Nothing built in the last fifteen or twenty years would have had a tank furnace installed. He'd want something in the city, wouldn't he?"

"Yeah, he'd want to be close to all of his marks. He wouldn't go for the 'burbs and even the boroughs aren't likely. Dave's a true urbanite and New York's his turf. Private home. Has to be. But how did he get his hands on a private residence?"

"Friends?" Roarke suggested. "Family?"

"Palmer didn't have a tight circle of friends. He's a loner. He has parents. They relocated after the trial. Went under the Victim and Survivor's Protection Act."

"Sealed files."

She heard the faintest trace of humor in his voice, turned to scowl at him. For a moment she wrestled with procedure. She could get clearance to access the Palmers' location.

And it would take at least two days to hack through the red tape for authorization. Or she could hand the problem to Roarke and have what she needed in minutes.

She could hear Stephanie Ring's screams echoing in her head.

"You'll have to use the unregistered equipment. Compuguard will have an automatic block on their file."

"It won't take long."

"I'm going to keep working on this." She gestured toward the screen. "He might have slipped up just enough to have let something identifiable come through."

"All right." But he crossed to her, framed her face in his hands. Lowering his head, he kissed her, long and slow and deep. And felt, as he did, some of the rigid tension in her body ease.

"I can handle this, Roarke."

"Whether you can or not, you will. Would it hurt to hold on to me, just for a minute?"

"Guess not." She slipped her arms around him, felt the familiar lines, the familiar warmth. Her grip tightened. "Why wasn't it enough to stop him once? Why wasn't it enough to put him away? What good is it if you do your job and it comes back this way?"

He held her and said nothing.

"He wants to show me he can do it all again. He wants to take me through all the steps and stages, the way he did before. Only this time as they're happening. 'Look how clever I am, Dallas.'"

"Knowing that, understanding that, will help you stop him a second time."

"Yeah." She eased back. "Get me the data so I can hammer at his parents."

Roarke skimmed a finger over the dent in her chin. "You'll let me watch, won't you. It's so stimulating to see you browbeat witnesses."

When she laughed, as he'd hoped she would, he went to his private room to circumvent Compuguard and officially sealed files.

She'd barely had time to review another section of the recording before he came back.

"It couldn't have been that easy."

"Yes." He smiled and passed her a new data disc. "It could. Thomas and Helen Palmer, now known as Thomas and Helen Smith — which shows just how imaginative bureaucrats can be, currently reside in a small town called Leesboro in rural Pennsylvania."

"Pennsylvania." Eve glanced toward her 'link, considered, then looked back at Roarke. "It wouldn't take long to get there if you had access to some slick transpo."

Roarke looked amused. "Which slick transpo would you prefer, Lieutenant?"

"That mini-jet of yours would get us there in under an hour."

"Then why don't we get started?"

If Eve had been more fond of heights, she might have enjoyed the fast, smooth flight south. As it was, she sat, jiggling a foot to relieve a case of nerves while Roarke piloted them over what she imagined some would consider a picturesque range of mountains.

To her they were just rocks, and the fields between them just dirt.

"I'm only going to say this once," she began. "And only because it's Christmas."

"Banking for landing," he warned her as he approached the private airstrip. "What are you only going to say once?"

"That maybe all these toys of yours aren't a complete waste of time. Overindulgent, maybe, but not a complete waste of time."

"Darling, I'm touched."

Once they were on the ground, they transferred from the snazzy little two-person jet to the car that Roarke had waiting. Of course, it couldn't be a normal vehicle, Eve mused as she studied it. It was a sleek black bullet of a car, built for style and speed.

"I'll drive." She held out a hand for the keycode the attendant had given him. "You navigate."

Roarke considered her as he tossed the code in his hand. "Why?"

"Because I'm the one with the badge." She snatched the code on its upward arc and smirked at him.

"I'm a better driver."

She snorted as they climbed in. "You like to hotdog. That doesn't make you better. Strap in, ace. I'm in a hurry."

She punched it and sent them flying away from the terminal and onto a winding rural road that was lined with snow-laced trees and sheer rock.

Roarke programmed their destination and studied the route offered by the onboard computer. "Follow this road for two miles, turn left for another ten point three, then next left for five point eight."

By the time he'd finished, she was already making the first left. She spotted a narrow creek, water fighting its way through ice, over rock. A scatter of houses, trees climbing steeply up hills, a few children playing with new airskates or boards in snow-covered yards.

"Why do people live in places like this? There's nothing here. You see all that sky?" she asked Roarke. "You shouldn't be able to see that much sky from down here. It can't be good for you. And where do they eat? We haven't passed a single restaurant, glide cart, deli, nothing."

"Cozily?" Roarke suggested. "Around the kitchen table."

"All the time? Jesus." She shuddered.

He laughed, smoothed a finger over her hair. "Eve, I adore you."

"Right." She tapped the brakes to make the next turn. "What am I looking for?"

"Third house on the right. There, that two-story prefab, mini-truck in the drive."

She slowed, scanning the house as she turned in behind the truck. There were Christmas lights along the eaves, a wreath on the door, and the outline of a decorated tree behind the front window.

"No point in asking you to wait in the car, I guess."

"None," he agreed and got out.

"They're not going to be happy to see me," Eve warned him as they crossed the shoveled walk to the front door. "If they refuse to talk to me, I'm going to give them some hard shoves. If it comes down to it, you just follow the lead."

She pressed the buzzer, shivered.

"You should have worn the coat I gave you. Cashmere's warm."

"I'm not wearing that on duty." It was gorgeous, she thought. And made her feel soft. It wasn't the sort of thing that worked for a cop.

And when the door opened, Eve was all cop.

Helen Palmer had changed her hair and her eyes. Subtle differences in shades and shapes, but enough to alter her looks. It was still a pretty face, very like her son's. Her automatic smile of greeting faded as she recognized Eve.

"You remember me, Mrs Palmer?"

"What are you doing here?" Helen put a hand high on the doorjamb as if to block it. "How did you find us? We're under protection."

"I don't intend to violate that. I have a crisis situation. You'd have been informed that your son has escaped from prison."

Helen pressed her lips together, hunched her shoulders as a defense against the cold that whipped through the open door. "They said they were looking for him, assured us that they'd have him back in custody, back in treatment very soon. He isn't here. He doesn't know where we are."

"Can I come in, Mrs Palmer?"

"Why do you have to rake this all up again?" Tears swam into her eyes, seeming as much from frustration as grief. "My husband and I are just getting our lives back. We've had no contact with David in nearly three years."

"Honey? Who's at the door? You're letting the cold in." A tall man with a dark sweep of hair came smiling to the door. He wore an old cardigan sweater and ancient jeans with a pair of obviously new slippers. He blinked once, twice, then laid his hand on his wife's shoulder. "Lieutenant. Lieutenant Dallas, isn't it?"

"Yes, Mr Palmer. I'm sorry to disturb you."

"Let them in, Helen."

"Oh, God, Tom."

"Let them in." His fingers rubbed over her shoulder before he drew her back. "You must be Roarke." Tom worked up what nearly passed for a smile as he offered

Roarke his hand. "I recognize you. Please come in and sit down."

"Tom, please —"

"Why don't you make some coffee?" He turned and pressed his lips to his wife's brow. He murmured something to her, and she let out a shuddering breath and nodded.

"I'll make this as quick as I can, Mr Palmer," Eve told him, as Helen walked quickly down a central hallway.

"You dealt very fairly with us during an unbearable time, Lieutenant." He showed them into a small living area. "I haven't forgotten that. Helen — my wife's been on edge all day. For several days," he corrected himself. "Since we were informed that David escaped. We've worked very hard to keep that out of the center, but . . ."

He gestured helplessly and sat down.

Eve remembered these decent people very well, their shock and grief over what their son was. They had raised him with love, with discipline, with care, and still they had been faced with a monster.

There had been no abuse, no cruelty, no underlying gruel for that monster to feed on. Mira's testing and analysis had corroborated Eve's impression of a normal couple who'd given their only child their affection and the monetary and social advantages that had been at their disposal.

"I don't have good news for you, Mr Palmer. I don't have easy news."

He folded his hands in his lap. "He's dead."

"No."

Tom closed his eyes. "God help me. I'd hoped — I'd actually hoped he was." He got up quickly when he heard his wife coming back. "Here, I'll take that." He bent to take the tray she carried. "We'll get through this, Helen."

"I know. I know we will." She came in, sat, busied herself pouring the coffee she'd made. "Lieutenant, do you think David's come back to New York?"

"We know he has." She hesitated, then decided they would hear the news soon enough through the media. "Early this morning the body of Judge Wainger was found in Rockefeller Plaza. It's David's work," she continued as Helen moaned. "He's contacted me, with proof. There's no doubt of it."

"He was supposed to be given treatment. Kept away from people so he couldn't hurt them, hurt himself."

"Sometimes the system fails, Mrs Palmer. Sometimes you can do everything right, and it just fails."

Helen rose, walked to the window, and stood looking out. "You said something like that to me before. To us. That we'd done everything right, everything we could. That it was something in David that had failed. That was kind of you, Lieutenant, but you can't know what it's like, you can't know how it feels to know that a monster has come from you."

No, Eve thought, but she knew what it was to come from a monster, to have been raised by one for the first eight years of her life. And she lived with it.

"I need your help," she said instead. "I need you to tell me if you have any idea where he might go, who he might go to. He has a place," she continued. "A private place where he can work. A house, a small building somewhere in New York. In the city or very close by."

"He has nowhere." Tom lifted his hands. "We sold everything when we relocated. Our home, my business, Helen's. Even our holiday place in the Hamptons. We cut all ties. The house where David — where he lived that last year — was sold as well. We live quietly here, simply. The money we'd accumulated, the money from the sales is sitting in an account. We haven't had the heart to . . . we don't need it."

"He had money of his own," Eve prompted.

"Yes, inheritance, a trust fund. It was how he financed what he was doing." Tom reached out a hand for his wife's and clasped her fingers tightly. "We donated that money to charity. Lieutenant, all the places where he might have gone are in the hands of others now."

"All right. You may think of something later. However far-fetched, please contact me." She rose. "When David's in custody again, I'll let you know. After that, I'll forget where you are."

Eve said nothing more until she and Roarke were in the car and headed back. "They still love him. After all he did, after what he is, there's a part of them that loves him."

"Yes, and enough, I think, to help you stop him, if they knew how."

"No one ever cared for us that way." She took her eyes off the road briefly, met his. "No one ever felt that bond."

"No." He brushed the hair from her cheek. "Not until we found each other. Don't grieve, Eve."

"He has his mother's eyes," she murmured. "Soft and blue and clear. She's the one who had to change them, I imagine, because she couldn't look in the mirror and face them every morning."

She signed, shook it off.

"But he can," she said quietly.

CHAPTER
FOUR

There was nothing else to do, no other data to examine or analyze, no other route to check. Tomorrow, she knew, there would be. Now she could only wait.

Eve walked into the bedroom with some idea of taking a catnap. They needed to salvage some of the day, she thought. To have their Christmas dinner together, to squeeze in some sense of normalcy.

The strong, dreamy scent of pine made her shake her head. The man had gone wild for tradition on this, their first Christmas together. Christ knew what he had paid for the live trees he'd placed throughout the house. And this one, the one that stood by the window in their bedroom, he'd insisted they decorate together.

It mattered to him. And with some surprise she realized it had come to matter to her.

"Tree lights on," she ordered, and smiled a little as she watched them blink and flash.

She stepped toward the seating area, released her weapon harness, and shrugged it off. She was sitting on the arm of the sofa taking off her boots when Roarke came in.

"Good. I was hoping you'd take a break. I've got some calls to make. Why don't you let me know when you're ready for a meal?"

She angled her head and studied him as he stood just inside the doorway. She let her second boot drop and stood up slowly. "Come here."

Recognizing the glint in her eyes, he felt the light tingle of lust begin to move through his blood. "There?"

"You heard me, slick."

Keeping his eyes on hers he walked across the room. "What can I do for you, Lieutenant?"

Traditions, Eve thought, had to start somewhere. She fisted a hand in the front of his shirt, straining the silk as she pulled him a step closer. "I want you naked, and quick. So unless you want me to get rough, strip."

His smile was as cocky as hers and made her want to sink in with her teeth. "Maybe I like it rough."

"Yeah?" She began to back him up toward the bed. "Well then, you're going to love this."

She moved fast, the only signal was the quick flash of her eyes before she ripped his shirt open and sent buttons flying. He gripped her hips, squeezing hard as she fixed her teeth on his shoulder and bit.

"Christ. Christ! I love your body. Give it to me."

"You want it?" He jerked her up to her toes. "You'll have to take it."

When his mouth would have closed hotly over hers, she pivoted. He countered. She came in low and might have flipped him if he hadn't anticipated her move.

They'd gone hand to hand before, with very satisfying results.

They ended face-to-face again, breath quickening. "I'm taking you down," she warned him.

"Try it."

They grappled, both refusing to give way. The momentum took them up the stairs of the platform to the bed. She slipped a hand between his legs, gently squeezed. It was a move she'd used before. Even as the heat shot straight down the center of his body to her palm, he shifted, slid under her guard, and flipped her onto the bed.

She rolled, came up in a crouch. "Come on, tough guy."

She was grinning now, her face flushed with battle, desire going gold in her eyes and the lights of the tree sparkling behind her.

"You look beautiful, Eve."

That had her blinking, straightening from the fighting stance and gaping at him. Even the man who loved her had never accused her of beauty. "Huh?"

It was all she managed before he leapt at her and took her out with a mid-body tackle.

"Bastard." She nearly giggled it even as she scissored up and managed to roll on top of him. But he used the impetus to keep going until he had her pinned again. "Beautiful, my ass."

"Your ass is beautiful." The elbow to his gut knocked some of the breath out of him, but he sucked more in. "And so's the rest of you. I'm going to have your beautiful ass, and the rest of you."

She bucked, twisted, nearly managed to slip out from under him. Then his mouth closed over her breast, sucking, nipping through her shirt. She moaned, arched up against him, and the fist she'd clenched in his hair dragged him closer rather than yanking him away.

When he tore at her shirt, she reared up, hooking strong, long legs around his waist, finding his mouth with hers again as he pushed back to kneel in the center of the bed.

They went over in a tangle of limbs, hands rough and groping. And flesh began to slide damply over flesh.

He took her up and over the first time, hard and fast, those clever fingers knowing her weaknesses, her strengths, her needs. Quivering, crying out, she let herself fly on the edgy power of the climax.

Then they were rolling again, gasps and moans and murmurs. Heat coming in tidal waves, nerves raw and needy. Her mouth was a fever on his as she straddled him.

"Let me, let me, let me." She chanted it against his mouth as she rose up. Her hands linked tight to his as she took him inside her. He filled her, body, mind, heart.

Fast and full of fury, she drove them both as she'd needed to from the moment he'd come into the room. It flooded into her, swelled inside her, that unspeakable pleasure, the pressure, the frantic war to end, to prolong.

She threw her head back, clung to it, that razor's edge. "Go over." She panted it out, fighting to clear her vision, to focus on that glorious face. "Go over first, and take me with you."

She watched his eyes, that staggering blue go dark as midnight, felt him leap over with one last, hard thrust. With her hands still locked in his, she threw herself over with him.

And when the energy slid away from her like wax from a melting candle, she slipped down, quivering even as she pressed her face into his neck.

"I won," she managed.

"Okay."

Her lips twitched at the smug, and exhausted, satisfaction in his voice. "I did. I got just what I wanted from you, pal."

"Thank Christ." He shifted until he could cradle her against him. "Take a nap, Eve."

"Just an hour." Knowing he would never sleep longer than that himself, she wrapped around him to keep him close.

When she woke at two A.M., Eve decided the brief pre-dinner nap had thrown her system off. Now she was fully awake, her mind engaged and starting to click through the information and evidence she had so far.

David Palmer was here, in New York. Somewhere out in the city, happily going about his work. And her gut told her Stephanie Ring was already dead.

He wouldn't have such an easy time getting to the others on his list, she thought as she turned in bed. Ego would push him to try, and he'd make a mistake. In all likelihood he'd already made one. She just hadn't picked up on it yet.

Closing her eyes, she tried to slip into Palmer's mind, as she had years before when she'd been hunting him.

He loved his work, had loved it even when he'd been a boy and doing his experiments on animals. He'd managed to hide those little deaths, to put on a bright, innocent face. Everyone who'd known him — parents, teachers, neighbors — had spoken of a cheerful, helpful boy, a bright one who studied hard and caused no trouble.

Yet some of the classic elements had been there, even in childhood. He'd been a loner, obsessively neat, compulsively organized. He'd never had a healthy sexual relationship and had been socially awkward with women. They'd found hundreds of journal discs, going back to his tenth year, carefully relating his theories, his goals, and his accomplishments.

And with time, with practice, with study, he'd gotten very, very good at his work.

Where would you set up, Dave? It would have to be somewhere comfortable. You like your creature comforts. You must have hated the lack of them in prison. Pissed you off, didn't it? So now you're coming after the ones who put you there.

That's a mistake, letting us know the marks in advance. But it's ego, too. It's really you against me.

That's another mistake, because no one knows you better.

A house, she thought. But not just any house. It would have to be in a good neighborhood, close to good restaurants. Those years of prison food must have offended your palate. You'd need furniture, comfortable stuff, with some style. Linens, good ones. And an entertainment complex — got to watch the screen or you won't know what people are saying about you.

And all that takes money.

When she sat up in bed, Roarke stirred beside her. "Figure it out?"

"He's got a credit line somewhere. I always wondered if he had money stashed, but it didn't seem to matter since he was never getting out to use it. I was wrong. Money's power, and he found a way to use it from prison."

She tossed back the duvet, started to leap out of bed when the 'link beeped. She stared at it a moment, and knew.

CHAPTER
FIVE

Two teenagers looking for a little adventure snuck out of their homes, met at a prearranged spot, and took their new scoot-bikes for a spin in Central Park.

They'd thought at first that Stephanie Ring was a vagrant, maybe a licensed beggar or a chemi-head sleeping it off, and they started to give her a wide berth.

But vagrants didn't make a habit of stretching out naked on the carousel in Central Park.

Eve had both of them stashed in a black-and-white. One had been violently ill, and the brittle air still carried the smear of vomit. She'd ordered the uniforms to set up a stand of lights so the area was under the glare of a false day.

Stephanie hadn't been beaten, nor had her hair been cut. Palmer believed in variety. There were dozens of long, thin slices over her arms and legs, the flesh around the wounds shriveled and discolored. Something toxic, Eve imagined, something that when placed on a relatively minor open wound would cause agony. The blood had been allowed to drip and dry. Her feet speared out at sharp angles, in a parody of a ballet stance. Dislocated.

Carved into her midriff were the signature block letters.

LET'S KILL ALL THE LAWYERS

He had finally killed this one, Eve thought, with the slow, torturous strangulation he was most fond of. Eve examined the noose, found the rope identical to that used on Judge Wainger.

Another mistake, Dave. Lots of little oversights this time around.

She reached for her field kit and began the routine that followed murder.

She went home to write her report, wanting the quiet she'd find there as opposed to the post-holiday confusion at Central. She shot a copy to her commander, then sent messages to both Peabody and Feeney. Once her aide and the top man in the Electronics Detective Division woke and checked their 'links, she was pulling them in.

She fueled on coffee, then set about the tedious task of peeling the layers from Palmer's financial records.

It was barely dawn when the door between her office and Roarke's opened. He came in, fully dressed, and she could hear the hum of equipment already at work in the room behind him.

"You working at home today?" she said it casually, sipping coffee as she studied him.

"Yes." He glanced down at her monitor. "Following the money, Lieutenant?"

"At the moment. You're not my bodyguard, Roarke."

He merely smiled. "And who, I wonder, could be more interested in your body?"

"I'm a cop. I don't need a sitter."

He reached down, cupped her chin. "What nearly happened to Peabody two nights ago?"

"It didn't happen. And I'm not having you hovering around when you should be off doing stuff."

"I can do stuff from here just as easily and efficiently as I can from midtown. You're wasting time arguing. And I doubt you'll find your money trail through Palmer's official records."

"I know it." The admission covered both statements, and frustrated her equally. "I have to start somewhere. Go away and let me work."

"Done with me, are you?" He lowered his head and brushed his lips over hers.

The sound of a throat being loudly and deliberately cleared came from the doorway. "Sorry." Peabody managed most of a smile. She was pale, and more than a little heavy-eyed, but her uniform was stiff and polished, as always.

"You're early." Eve rose, then slid her hands awkwardly into her pockets.

"The message said to report as soon as possible."

"I'll leave you two to work." Alone, Roarke thought, the two of them would slip past the discomfort faster. "It's good to see you, Peabody. Lieutenant," he added before he closed the door between the rooms, "you might want to check the names of deceased relatives. The transfer and disbursement of funds involving accounts with the same last name and blood ties are rarely noticed."

"Yeah, right. Thanks." Eve shifted her feet. The last time she'd seen her aide, Peabody had been wrapped in a blanket, her face blotchy from tears. "You okay?"

"Yeah, mostly."

Mostly, my ass, Eve thought. "Look, I shouldn't have called you in on this. Take a couple of more days to level off."

"Sir. I'd do better if I got back to work, into routine. Sitting home watching videos and eating soy chips isn't the way I want to spend another day. Work clears it out quicker."

Because she believed that herself, Eve moved her shoulders. "Then get some coffee, Peabody, I've got plenty of work here."

"Yes, sir." She stepped forward, pulling a small wrapped box from her pocket, setting it on the desk as she went to the AutoChef. "Your Christmas present. I didn't get a chance to give it to you before."

"I guess we were a little busy." Eve toyed with the ribbon. Gifts always made her feel odd, but she could sense Peabody's eyes on her. She ripped off the red foil, opened the lid. It was a silver star, a little dented, a bit discolored.

"It's an old sheriff's badge," Peabody told her. "I don't guess it's like Wyatt Earp's or anything, but it's official. I thought you'd get a kick out of it. You know, the long tradition of law and order."

Absurdly touched, Eve grinned. "Yeah. It's great." For the fun of it, she took it out and pinned it to her shirt. "Does this make you the deputy?"

"It suits you, Dallas. You'd've stood up wherever, whenever."

Looking up, Eve met her eyes. "You stand, Peabody. I wouldn't have called you in today if I thought different."

"I guess I needed to hear that. Thanks. Well . . ." She hesitated, then lifted her brows in question.

"Problem?"

"No, I just . . ." She pouted, giving her square, sober face a painfully young look. "Hmmm."

"You didn't like your present?" Eve said lightly. "You'll have to take that up with Leonardo."

"What present? What's he got to do with it?"

"He made that wardrobe for your undercover work. If you don't like it . . ."

"The clothes." Like magic, Peabody's face cleared. "I get to keep all those mag clothes? All of them?"

"What the hell am I supposed to do with them? Now are you going to stand around grinning like an idiot or can I get on with things here?"

"I can grin and work at the same time, sir."

"Settle down. Start a run and trace on this rope." She pushed a hard-copy description across the desk. "I want any sales within the last week, bulk sales. He uses a lot of it."

"Who?"

"We'll get to that. Run the rope, then get me a list of private residences — upscale — sold or rented in the metro area within the last week. Also private luxury vehicles — pickup or delivery on those within the last week. He needs transpo and he'd go classy. The cage," she muttered as she began to pace. "Where the hell did he get the cage? Wildlife facility, domestic animal detention? We'll track it. Start the runs, Peabody, I'll brief you when Feeney gets here."

She'd called in Feeney, Peabody thought as she sat down at a computer. It was big. Just what she needed.

"You'll both want to review the investigation discs, profiles, transcripts from the Palmer case of three years ago. Feeney," Eve added, "you'll remember most of it. You tracked and identified the electronic equipment he used in those murders."

"Yeah, I remember the little bastard." Feeney sat scowling into his coffee. His habitually weary face was topped by wiry red hair that never seemed to decide which direction it wanted to take.

He was wearing a blue shirt, so painfully pressed and bright that Eve imagined it had come out of its gift box only that morning. And would be comfortably rumpled by afternoon.

"Because we know him, his pattern, his motives, and in this case his victims or intended victims, he's given us an edge. He knows that, enjoys that because he's sure he'll be smarter."

"He hates you, Dallas." Feeney's droopy eyes lifted, met hers. "He hated your ever-fucking guts all along. You stopped him, then you played him until he spilled everything. He'll come hard for you."

"I hope you're right, because I want the pleasure of taking him out again. He got the first two on his list because he had a lead on us," she continued. "The others have been notified, warned, and are under guard. He may or may not make an attempt to continue in order. But once he runs into a snag, he'll skip down."

"And come for you," Peabody put in.

"Everything the others did happened because I busted him. Under the whack is a very logical mind. Everything he does has a reason. It's his reason, so it's bent — but it's there."

She glanced at her wrist unit. "I've got a meeting with Mira at her residence in twenty minutes. I'm going to leave it to Feeney to fill you in on any holes in this briefing, Peabody. Once you have the lists from the runs I ordered, do a probability scan. See if we can narrow the field a bit. Feeney, when you review the disc he sent through Nadine, you might be able to tag some of the equipment. You get a line on it, we can trace the source. We do it in steps, but we do it fast. If he misses on the list, he might settle for someone else, anyone else. He's been out a week and already killed twice."

She broke off as her communicator signaled. She walked to retrieve her jacket as she answered. Two minutes later she jammed it back in her pocket. And her eyes were flat and cold.

"Make that three times. He got to Carl Neissan."

Eve was still steaming when she rang the bell of Mira's dignified brownstone. The fact that the guard on door duty demanded that she show her ID and had it verified before entry mollified her slightly. If the man posted at Neissan's had done the same, Palmer wouldn't have gotten inside.

Mira came down the hall toward her. She was dressed casually in slacks and sweater, with soft matching shoes. But there was nothing casual about her eyes. Before Eve could speak, she lifted a hand.

"I appreciate your coming here. We can talk upstairs in my office." She glanced to the right as a child's laughter bounced through an open doorway. "Under different circumstances I'd introduce you to my family. But I'd rather not put them under any more stress."

"We'll leave them out of it."

"I wish that were possible." Saying nothing more, Mira started upstairs.

The house reflected her, Eve decided. Calming colors, soft edges, perfect style. Her home office was half the size of her official one and must at one time have been a small bedroom. Eve noted that she'd furnished it with deep chairs and what she thought of as a lady's desk, with curved legs and fancy carving.

Mira adjusted the sunscreen on a window and turned to the mini AutoChef recessed into the wall.

"You'll have reviewed my original profile on David Palmer," she began, satisfied that her hands were steady as she programmed for tea. "I would stand by it, with a few additions due to his time in prison."

"I didn't come for a profile. I've got him figured."

"Do you?"

"I walked around inside his head before. We both did."

"Yes." Mira offered Eve a delicate cup filled with the fragrant tea they both knew she didn't want. "In some ways he remains the exception to a great many rules. He had a loving and advantaged childhood. Neither of his parents exhibits any signs of emotional or psychological defects. He did well in school, more of an overachiever than under-, but nothing off the scale. Testing showed no brain deformities, no physical abnormalities. There is no psychological or physiological root for his condition."

"He likes it," Eve said briefly. "Sometimes evil's its own root."

"I want to disagree," Mira murmured. "The reasons, the whys of abnormal behavior are important to me. But I have no reasons, no whys, for David Palmer."

"That's not your problem, Doctor. Mine is to stop him, and to protect the people he's chosen. The first two on his list are dead."

"Stephanie Ring? You're sure."

"Her body was found this morning. Carl Neissan's been taken."

This time Mira's hand shook, rattling her cup in its saucer before she set it aside. "He was under guard."

"Palmer got himself into a cop suit, knocked on the damn door, and posed as the relief. The on-duty didn't question it. He went home to a late Christmas dinner. When the morning duty came on, he found the house empty."

"And the night relief? The real one?"

"Inside the trunk of his unit. Tranq'd and bound but otherwise unharmed. He hasn't come around enough to be questioned yet. Hardly matters. We know it was Palmer. I'm arranging for Justine Polinsky to be moved to a safe house. You'll want to pack some things, Doctor. You're going under."

"You know I can't do that, Eve. This is as much my case as yours."

"You're wrong. You're a consultant, and that's it. I don't need consultation. I'm no longer confident that you can be adequately protected in this location. I'm moving you."

"Eve —"

"Don't fuck with me." It came out sharp, very close to mean, and Mira jerked back in surprise. "I'm taking you into police custody. You can gather up some personal things or you can go as you are. But you're going."

Calling on the control that ran within her like her own bloodstream, Mira folded her hands in her lap. "And you? Will you be going under?"

"I'm not your concern."

"Of course you are, Eve," Mira said quietly, watching the storm of emotions in Eve's eyes. "Just as I'm yours. And my family downstairs is mine. They're not safe."

"I'll see to it. I'll see to them."

Mira nodded, closed her eyes briefly. "It would be a great relief to me to know they were away from here, and protected. It's difficult for me to cope when I'm worried about their welfare."

"He won't touch them. I promise you."

"I'll take your word. Now as to my status —"

"I didn't give you multiple choices, Dr Mira."

"Just a moment." Composed again, Mira picked up her tea. "I think you'll agree . . . I have every bit as much influence with your superiors as you do. It would hardly serve either of us to play at tugging strings. I'm not being stubborn or courageous," she added. "Those are your traits."

A ghost of a smile curved her mouth when Eve frowned at her. "I admire them. You're also a woman who can see past emotion to the goal. The goal is to stop David Palmer. I can be of use. We both know it. With my family away I'll be less distracted. And I can't be with them, Eve, because if I am I'll worry that he'll harm one of them to get to me."

She paused for a moment, judged that Eve was considering. "I have no argument to having guards here or at my office. In fact, I want them. Very much. I have no intention of taking any unnecessary chances or risks. I'm just asking you to let me do my work."

"You can do your work where I put you."

"Eve." Mira drew a breath. "If you put both me and Justine out of his reach, there's the very real possibility he'll take someone else." She nodded. "You've considered that already. He won't come for you until he's ready. You're the grand prize. If no one else is accessible, he'll strike out. He'll want to keep to his timetable, even if it requires a substitute."

"I've got some lines on him."

"And you'll find him. But if he believes I'm accessible, if I'm at least visible, he'll be satisfied to focus his energies on getting through. I expect you to prevent that." She smiled again, easier now. "And I intend to do everything I can to help you."

"I can make you go. All your influence won't matter if I toss you in restraints and have you hauled out of here. You'll be pissed off, but you'll be safe."

"I wouldn't put it past you," Mira agreed. "But you know I'm right."

"I'm doubling your guards. You're wearing a bracelet. You work here. You're not to leave the house for any reason." Her eyes flashed when Mira started to protest. "You push me on this, you're going to find out what it feels like to wear cuffs." Eve rose. "Your guards will do hourly check-ins. Your 'link will be monitored."

"That hardly makes me appear accessible."

"He'll know you're here. That's going to have to be enough. I've got work to do." Eve started for the door, hesitated, then spoke without turning around. "Your family, they matter to you."

"Yes, of course."

"You matter to me." She walked away quickly, before Mira could get shakily to her feet.

CHAPTER
SIX

Eve headed to the lab from Mira's. From there she planned a stop by the morgue and another at Carl Neissan's before returning to her home office.

Remembering Mira's concern about family, Eve called Roarke on her palm-link after she parked and started into the building.

"Why are you alone?" was the first thing he said to her.

"Cut it out." She flashed her badge at security, then headed across the lobby and down toward the labs. "I'm in a secured facility, surrounded by rent-a-cops, monitors, and lab dorks. I've got a job to do. Let me do it."

"He's gotten three out of six."

She stopped, rolled her eyes. "Oh, I get it. Shows what kind of faith you have in me. I guess being a cop for ten years makes me as easy a fish as a seventy-year-old judge and a couple of soft lawyers."

"You annoy me, Eve."

"Why? Because I'm right?"

"Yes. And snotty about it." But his smile warmed a little. "Why did you call?"

"So I could be snotty. I'm at the lab, about to tackle Dickhead. I've got a few stops to make after this. I'll check in."

It was a casual way to let him know she understood he worried. And he accepted, in the same tone. "I've several 'link conferences this afternoon. Call in on the private line. Watch your back, Lieutenant. I'm very fond of it."

Satisfied, she swung into the lab. Dickie, the chief tech, was there, looking sleepy-eyed and pale as he stared at the readout on his monitor.

The last time she'd been in the lab, there'd been a hell of a party going on. Now those who'd bothered to come in worked sluggishly and looked worse.

"I need reports, Dickie. Wainger and Ring."

"Jesus, Dallas." He looked up mournfully, hunching his shoulders. "Don't you ever stay home?"

Since he looked ill, she gave him a little leeway. Silently she opened her jacket, tapped the silver star pinned to her shirt. "I'm the law," she said soberly. "The law has no home."

It made him grin a little, then he moaned. "Man, I got the mother of all Christmas hangovers."

"Mix yourself up a potion, Dickie, and get over it. Dave's got number three."

"Dave who?"

"Palmer, David Palmer." She resisted letting out her impatience by cuffing him on the side of the head. But she imagined doing it. "Did you read the damn directive?"

"I've only been here twenty minutes. Jesus." He rolled his shoulders, rubbed his face, drew in three sharp nasal breaths. "Palmer? That freak's caged."

"Not anymore. He skipped and he's back in New York. Wainger and Ring are his."

"Shit. Damn shit." He didn't look any less ill, but his eyes were alert now. "Fucking Christmas week and we get the world's biggest psycho-freak."

"Yeah, and Happy New Year, too. I need the results, on the rope, on the paper. I want to know what he used to carve the letters. You get any hair or fiber from the sweepers?"

"No, wait, just wait a damn minute." He scooted his rolling chair down the counter, barked orders at a computer, muttering as he scanned the data. "Bodies were clean. No hair other than victim's. No fiber."

"He always kept them clean," Eve murmured.

"Yeah, I remember. I remember. Got some dust — like grit between the toes, both victims."

"Concrete dust."

"Yeah. Get you the grade, possible age. Now the rope." He skidded back. "I was just looking at it, just doing the test run. Nothing special or exotic about it. Standard nylon strapping rope. Give me some time, I'll get you the make."

"How much time?"

"Two hours, three tops. Takes longer when it's standard."

"Make it fast." She swung away. "I'm in the field."

★ ★ ★

She stopped at the morgue next, to harass the chief medical examiner. It was more difficult to intimidate Morse or to rush him.

No sexual assault or molestation, no mutilation or injuries of genitalia.

Typical of Palmer, Eve thought as she ran over Morse's prelim report in her head. He was as highly asexual as anyone she'd come up against. She doubted that he even thought of the gender of his victims other than as a statistic for his experiments.

Subject Wainger's central nervous system had been severely damaged. Subject suffered minor cardiac infarction during abduction and torture period. Anus and interior of mouth showed electrical burns. Both hands crushed with a smooth, heavy instrument. Three ribs cracked.

The list of injuries went on until Morse had confirmed the cause of death as strangulation. And the time of death as midnight, December twenty-fourth.

She spent an hour at Carl Neissan's, another at Wainger's. In both cases, she thought, the door had been opened, Palmer allowed in. He was good at that. Good at putting on a pretty smile and talking his way in.

He looked so damn innocent, Eve thought as she climbed the steps to her own front door. Even the eyes — and the eyes usually told you — were those of a young, harmless man. They hadn't flickered, hadn't glazed or brightened, even when he'd sat in interview across from her and described each and every murder.

They'd taken on the light of madness only when he talked about the scope and importance of his work.

64

"Lieutenant." Summerset, tall and bony in severe black, slipped out of a doorway. "Do I assume your guests will be remaining for lunch?"

"Guests? I don't have any guests." She stripped off her jacket, tossed it across the newel post. "If you mean my team, we'll deal with it."

He had the jacket off the post even as she started up the stairs. At his low growl of disgust she glanced back. He held in his fingertips the gloves she'd balled into her jacket pocket. "What have you done to these?"

"It's just sealant." Which she'd forgotten to clean off before she shoved them into her pocket.

"These are handmade, Italian leather with mink lining."

"Mink? Shit. What is he, crazy?" Shaking her head, she kept on going. "Mink lining, for Christ's sake. I'll have lost them by next week, then some stupid mink will have died for nothing." She glanced down the hallway at Roarke's office door, shook her head again, and walked into her own.

She was right, Eve noted. Her team could deal with lunch on their own. Feeney was chowing down on some kind of multitiered sandwich while he muttered orders into the computer and scanned. Peabody had a deep bowl of pasta, scooping it up one-handed, sliding printouts into a pile with the other.

Her office smelled like an upscale diner and sounded like cops. Computer and human voices clashed, the printer hummed, and the main 'link was beeping and being ignored.

She strode over and answered it herself. "Dallas."

"Hey, got your rope." When she saw Dickie shove a pickle in his mouth, she wondered if every city official's stomach had gone on alarm at the same time. "Nylon strapping cord, like I said. This particular type is top grade, heavy load. Manufactured by Kytell outta Jersey. You guys run the distributor, that's your end."

"Yeah. Thanks." She broke transmission, thinking Dickie wasn't always a complete dickhead. He'd come through and hadn't required a bribe.

"Lieutenant," Peabody began, but Eve held up a finger and walked to Roarke's door and through it. "Do you own Kytell in New Jersey?"

Then she stopped and winced when she saw that he was in the middle of a holographic conference. Several images turned, studied her out of politely annoyed eyes.

"Sorry."

"It's all right. Gentlemen, ladies, this is my wife." Roarke leaned back in his chair, monumentally amused that Eve had inadvertently made good on her threat to barge in on one of his multimillion-dollar deals just to annoy him. "If you'd excuse me one moment. Caro?"

The holo of his administrative assistant rose, smiled. "Of course. We'll shift to the boardroom momentarily." The image turned, ran her hands over controls that only she could see, and the holos winked away.

"I should have knocked or something."

"It's not a problem. They'll hold. I'm about to make them all very rich. Do I own what?"

"Did you have to say 'my wife' that way, like I'd just run up from the kitchen?"

"So much more serene an image than telling them you'd just ran in from the morgue. And it is a rather conservative company I'm about to buy. Now, do I own what and why do you want to know?"

"Kytell, based in New Jersey. They make rope."

"Do they? Well, I have no idea. Just a minute." He swiveled at the console, asked for the information on the company. Which, Eve thought with some irritation, she could have damn well done herself.

"Yes, they're an arm of Yancy, which is part of Roarke Industries. And which, I assume, made the murder weapon."

"Right the first time."

"Then you'll want the distributor, the stores in the New York area where large quantities were sold to one buyer within the last week."

"Peabody can get it."

"I'll get it faster. Give me thirty minutes to finish up in here, then I'll shoot the data through to your unit."

"Thanks." She started out, turned back. "The third woman on the right? The redhead? She was giving you a leg shot — another inch of skirt lift and it would have been past her crotch."

"I noticed. Very nice legs." He smiled. "But she still won't get more than eighty point three a share. Anything else?"

"She's no natural redhead," Eve said for the hell of it and heard him laugh as she shut the door between them.

"Sir." Peabody got to her feet. "I think I have a line on the vehicle. Three possibles, high-end privates sold to single men in their early to mid-twenties on December twentieth and twenty-first. Two dealerships on the East Side and one in Brooklyn."

"Print hard copies of Palmer's photo."

"Already done."

"Feeney?"

"Whittling it down."

"Keep whittling. Roarke should have some data on the murder weapon inside a half hour. Send what he has to me in the field, will you? Peabody, you're with me."

The first dealership was a wash, and as she pulled up at the second, Eve sincerely hoped she didn't have to head to Brooklyn. The shiny new vehicles on the showroom floor had Peabody's eyes gleaming avariciously. Only Eve's quick elbow jab kept her from stroking the hood of a Booster-6Z, the sport-utility vehicle of the year.

"Maintain some dignity," Eve muttered. She flagged a salesman, who looked none too happy when she flipped out her badge. "I need to talk to the rep who sold a rig like this" — she gestured toward the Booster — "last week. Young guy bought it."

"Lana sold one of the 6Zs a few days before Christmas." Now he looked even unhappier. "She often rounds up the younger men." He pointed to a woman at a desk on the far side of the showroom.

"Thanks." Eve walked over, noting that Lana had an explosion of glossy black curls cascading down her back, a headset over it, and was fast-talking a potential customer on the line while she manually operated a keyboard with fingernails painted a vivid red.

"I can put you in it for eight a month. Eight a month and you're behind the wheel of the sexiest, most powerful land and air unit currently produced. I'm slicing my commission to the bone because I want to see you drive off in what makes you happy."

"Make him happy later, Lana." Eve held her badge in front of Lana's face.

Lana put a hand over the mouthpiece, studied the ID, cursed softly. Then her voice went back to melt. "Jerry, you take one more look at the video, try out the holo run. If you're not smiling by the end of it, the 7000's not the one for you. You call me back and let me know. Remember, I want you happy. Hear?"

She disconnected, glared at Eve. "I paid those damn parking violations. Every one."

"Glad to hear it. Our city needs your support. I need information on a sale you made last week. Booster. You were contacted earlier today and confirmed."

"Yeah, right. Nice guy, pretty face." She smiled. "He knew what he wanted right off."

"Is this the guy?" Eve signaled to Peabody, who took out the photo.

"Yeah. Cute."

"Yeah, he's real cute. I need the data. Name, address, the works."

"Sure, no problem." She turned to her machine, asked for the readout. Then, looking back up at Eve, she narrowed her eyes. "You look familiar. Have I sold you a car?"

Eve thought of her departmental issue, its sad pea-green finish and blocky style. "No."

"You really look — Oh!" Lana lit up like a Christmas tree. "Sure, sure, you're Roarke's wife. Roarke's cop wife. I've seen you on screen. Word is he's got an extensive collection of vehicles. Where does he deal?"

"Wherever he wants," Eve said shortly, and Lana let out a gay laugh.

"Oh, I'm sure he does. I'd absolutely love to show him our brand-new Barbarian. It won't be on the market for another three months, but I can arrange a private showing. If you'd just give him my card, Mrs Roarke, I'll be —"

"You see this?" Eve took out her badge again, all but pushed it into Lana's pert nose. "It says 'Dallas.' Lieutenant Dallas. I'm not here to liaison your next commission. This is an official investigation. Give me the damn data."

"Certainly. Of course." If her feathers were ruffled, Lana hid it well. "Um, the name is Peter Nolan, 123 East Sixty-eighth, apartment 4-B."

"How'd he pay?"

"That I remember. Straight E-transfer. The whole shot. Didn't want to finance. The transfer was ordered, received, and confirmed, and he drove off a happy man."

"I need all the vehicle information, including temp license and registration number. Full description."

"All right. Gee, what'd he do? Kill somebody?"

"Yeah, he did."

"Wow." Lana busily copied the data disc. "You just can't trust a pretty face," she said and slipped her business card into the disc pack.

CHAPTER
SEVEN

Peter Nolan didn't live at the Sixty-eighth Street address. The Kowaskis, an elderly couple, and their creaky schnauzer had lived there for fifteen years.

A check of the bank showed that the Nolan account had been opened, in person, on December 20 of that year and closed on December 22.

Just long enough to do the deal, Eve thought. But where had he gotten the money?

Taking Roarke's advice, she rounded out a very long day by starting searches on accounts under the name of Palmer. It would, she thought, rubbing her eyes, take a big slice of time.

How much time did Carl have? she wondered. Another day, by her guess. If Palmer was running true to form, he would begin to enjoy his work too much to rush through it. But sometime within the next twenty-four hours, she believed he'd try for Justine Polinsky.

While her machine worked, she leaned back and closed her eyes. Nearly midnight, she thought. Another day. Feeney was working his end. She was confident they'd have a line on the equipment soon, then there were the houses to check. They had the make, model, and license of his vehicle.

He'd left a trail, she thought. He wanted her to follow it, wanted her close. The son of a bitch.

It's you and me, isn't it, Dave? she thought as her mind started to drift. How fast can I be, and how clever? You figure it'll make it all the sweeter when you've got me in that cage. It's because you want that so bad that you're making mistakes. Little mistakes.

I'm going to hang you with them.

She slid into sleep while her computer hummed and woke only when she felt herself being lifted.

"What?" Reflexively she reached for the weapon she'd already unharnessed.

"You need to be in bed." Roarke held her close as he left the office.

"I was just resting my eyes. I've got data coming in. Don't carry me."

"You were dead out, the data will be there in the morning, and I'm already carrying you."

"I'm getting closer, but not close enough."

He'd seen the financial data on her screen. "I'll take a look through the accounts in the morning," he told her as he laid her on the bed.

"I've got it covered."

He unpinned her badge, set it aside. "Yes, Sheriff, but money is my business. Close it down a while."

"He'll be sleeping now." She let Roarke undress her. "In a big, soft bed with clean sheets. Dave likes to be clean and comfortable. He'll have a monitor in the bedroom so he can watch Neissan. He likes to watch before he goes to sleep. He told me."

"Don't think." Roarke slipped into bed beside her, gathered her close.

"He wants me."

"Yes, I know." Roarke pressed his lips to her hair as much to comfort himself as her. "But he can't have you."

Sleep helped. She'd dropped into it like a stone and had lain on the bottom of the dreaming pool for six hours. There'd been no call in the middle of the night to tell her Carl Neissan's body had been found.

Another day, she thought again and strode into her office. Roarke was at her desk, busily screening data.

"What are you doing?" She all but leapt to him. "That's classified."

"Don't pick nits, darling. You were going too broad last night. You'll be days compiling and rejecting all accounts under the name Palmer. You want one that shows considerable activity, large transfers, and connections to other accounts — which is, of course, the trickier part if you're dealing with someone who understands how to hide the coin."

"You can't just sit down and start going through data accumulated in an investigation."

"Of course I can. You need coffee." He looked up briefly. "Then you'll feel more yourself and I'll show you what I have."

"I feel exactly like myself." Which, she admitted, at the moment was annoyed and edgy. She stalked to the AutoChef in the kitchen, went for an oversized mug of hot and black. The rich and real caffeine Roarke could command zipped straight through her system.

"What have you got?" she demanded when she walked back in.

"Palmer was too simple, too obvious," Roarke began, and she narrowed her eyes.

"You didn't think so yesterday."

"I said check for relatives, same names. I should have suggested you try his mother's maiden name. Riley. And here we have the account of one Palmer Riley. It was opened six years ago, standard brokerage account, managed. Since there's been some activity over the last six months, I would assume your man found a way to access a 'link or computer from prison."

"He shouldn't have been near one. How can you be sure?"

"He understands how money works, and just how fluid it can be. You see here that six months ago he had a balance of just over $1.3 million. For the past three years previous, all action was automatic, straight managed with no input from the account holder. But here he begins to make transfers. Here's one to an account under Peter Nolan, which, by the way, is his aunt's husband's name on his father's side. Overseas accounts, off-planet accounts, local New York accounts — different names, different IDs. He's had this money for some time and he waited, sat on it until he found the way to use it."

"When I took him down before, we froze his accounts, accounts under David Palmer. We didn't look deeper. I didn't think of it."

"Why should you have? You stopped him, you put him away. He was meant to stay away."

"If I'd cleared it all, he wouldn't have had the backing to come back here."

"Eve, he'd have found a way." He waited until she looked at him. "You know that."

"Yeah." She let out a long breath. "Yeah, I know that. This tells me he's been planning, he's been shopping, he's been juggling funds, funneling into cover accounts. I need to freeze them. I don't think a judge is going to argue with me, not after what happened to one of their own."

"You'll piss him off."

"That's the plan. I need the names, numbers, locations of all the accounts you can connect to him." She blew out a breath. "Then I guess I owe you."

"Use your present, and we'll call it even."

"My present? Oh, yeah. Where and/or when do I want to go for a day. Let me mull that over a little bit. We get this wrapped, I'll use it for New Year's Eve."

"There's a deal."

A horrible thought snuck into her busy mind. "We don't have like a thing for New Year's, do we? No party or anything."

"No. I didn't want anything but you."

She looked back at him, narrowing her eyes even as the smile spread. "Do you practice saying stuff like that?"

"No." He rose, framed her face and kissed her, hard and deep. "I have all that stuff on disc."

"You're a slick guy, Roarke." She skimmed her fingers through her hair and simply lost herself for a

76

moment in the look of him. Then, giving herself a shake, she stepped back. "I have to work."

"Wait." He grabbed her hand before she could turn away. "What was that?"

"I don't know. It just comes over me sometimes. You, I guess, come over me sometimes. I don't have time for it now."

"Darling Eve." He brushed his thumb over her knuckles. "Be sure to make time later."

"Yeah, I'll do that."

They worked together for an hour before Peabody arrived. She switched gears, leaving Roarke to do what he did best — manipulate data — while she focused on private residences purchased in the New York area, widening the timing to the six months since Palmer had activated his account.

Feeney called in to let her know he'd identified some of the equipment from the recording and was following up.

Eve gathered her printouts and rose. "We've got more than thirty houses to check. Have to do it door-to-door since I don't trust the names and data. He could have used anything. Peabody —"

"I'm with you, sir."

"Right. Roarke, I'll be in the field."

"I'll let you know when I have this wrapped."

She looked at him, working smoothly, thoroughly, methodically. And wondered who the hell was dealing with what she often thought of as his empire. "Look, I can call a man in for this. McNab —"

"McNab." Peabody winced at the name before she could stop herself. She had a temporary truce going with the EDD detective, but that didn't mean she wanted to share her case with him. Again. "Dallas, come on. It's been so nice and quiet around here."

"I've got this." Roarke shot her a glance, winked at Peabody. "I have an investment in it now."

"Whatever. Shoot me, and Feeney, the data when you have it all. I'm going to check out the rope, too. He likely picked up everything himself, but it would only take one delivery to pin down his hole."

After three hours of knocking on doors, questioning professional parents, housekeepers, or others who chose the work-at-home route, Eve took pity on Peabody and swung by a glide cart.

In this neighborhood the carts were clean, the awnings or umbrellas bright, the operators polite. And the prices obscene.

Peabody winced as she was forced to use a credit card for nothing but coffee, a kabob, and a small scoop of paper-thin oil chips.

"It's my metabolism," she muttered as she climbed back into the car. "I have one that requires fuel at regular intervals."

"Then pump up," Eve advised. "It's going to be a long day. At least half these people aren't going to be home until after the five o'clock shift ends."

She snagged the 'link when it beeped. "Dallas."

"Hello, Lieutenant." Roarke eyed her soberly. "Your data's coming through."

"Thanks. I'll start on the warrant."

"One thing — I didn't find any account with a withdrawal or transfer that seemed large enough for a purchase or down payment on a house. A couple are possible, but if, as you told me, he didn't finance a car, it's likely he didn't want to deal with the credit and Compuguard checks on his rating and background."

"He's got a damn house, Roarke. I know it."

"I'm sure you're right. I'm not convinced he acquired it recently."

"I've still got twenty-couple to check," she replied. "I have to follow through on that. Maybe he's just renting. He likes to own, but maybe this time he's renting. I'll run it through that way, too."

"There weren't any standard transfers or withdrawals that would indicate rent or mortgage payments."

She hissed out a breath. "It's ridiculous."

"What?"

"How good a cop you'd make."

"I don't think insulting me is appropriate under the circumstances. I have some business of my own to tend to," he said when she grinned at him. "I'll get back to yours shortly."

Palmer had purchased, and personally picked up, a hundred twenty yards of nylon rope from a supply warehouse store off Canal. The clerk who had handled the sale ID'd the photo and mentioned what a nice young man Mr Dickson had been. As Dickson, Palmer had also purchased a dozen heavy-load pulleys, a supply of steel O rings, cable, and the complete Handy

Homemaker set of Steelguard tools, including the accessory laser package.

The entire business had been loaded into the cargo area of his shiny new Booster-6Z — which the clerk had admired — on the morning of December 22.

Eve imagined Palmer had been a busy little bee that day and throughout the next, setting up his private chamber of horrors.

By eight they'd eliminated all the houses on Eve's initial list.

"That's it." Eve climbed back in her vehicle and pressed her fingers to her eyes. "They all check out. I'll drop you at a transpo stop, Peabody."

"Are you going home?"

Eve lowered her hands. "Why?"

"Because I'm not going off duty if you're starting on the list of rentals I ran."

"Excuse me?"

Peabody firmed her chin. Eve could arrow a cold chill up your spine when she took on that superior-officer tone. "I'm not going off duty, sir, to leave you solo in the field with Palmer on the loose and you as a target. With respect, Lieutenant."

"You don't think I can handle some little pissant, mentally defective?"

"I think you want to handle him too much." Peabody sucked in a breath. "I'm sticking, Dallas."

Eve narrowed her eyes. "Have you been talking to Roarke?" At the quick flicker in Peabody's eyes Eve swore. "Goddamn it."

80

"He's right and you're wrong. Sir." Peabody braced for the explosion, was determined to weather it, then all but goggled with shock.

"Maybe," was all Eve said as she pulled away from the curb.

Since she was on a roll, Peabody slanted Eve a look. "You haven't eaten all day. You didn't even steal any of my oil chips. You could use a meal."

"Okay, okay. Christ, Roarke's got your number, doesn't he?"

"I wish."

"Zip it, Peabody. We'll fuel the metabolism, then start on the rental units."

"Zipping with pleasure, sir."

CHAPTER
EIGHT

It began to snow near midnight, fat, cold flakes with icy edges. Eve watched it through the windshield and told herself it was time to stop. The night was over. Nothing more could be done.

"He's got all the cards," she murmured.

"You've got a pretty good hand, Dallas." Peabody shifted in her seat, grateful for the heat of the car. Even her bones were chilled.

"Doesn't matter what I've got." Eve drove away from the last rental unit they'd checked. "Not tonight. I know who he is, who he's going to kill. I know how he does it and I know why. And tonight it doesn't mean a damn thing. Odds are, he's done with Carl now."

It was rare to see Eve discouraged. Angry, yes, Peabody thought with some concern. And driven. But she couldn't recall ever hearing that quiet resignation in her lieutenant's voice before. "You covered all the angles. You took all the steps."

"That's not going to mean much to Carl. And if I'd covered all the angles, I'd have the son of a bitch. So I'm missing one. He's slipping through because I can't pin it."

"You've only had the case for three days."

"No. I've had it for three years." As she pulled up at a light, her 'link beeped. "Dallas."

"Lieutenant, this is Detective Dalrymple, assigned to observation on the Polinsky residence. We've got a mixed-race male, mid-twenties, average height and build. Subject is on foot and carrying a small sack. He used what appeared to be a key code to gain access to premises. He's inside now."

"I'm three blocks east of your location and on my way." She'd already whipped around the corner. "Secure all exits, call for backup. Doesn't make sense," she muttered to Peabody as they barreled across Madison. "Right out in the open? Falls right into our laps? Doesn't fucking make sense."

She squealed to a stop a half a block from the address. Her weapon was in her hand before she hit the sidewalk. "Peabody, the Polinsky unit is on four, south side. Go around, take the fire escape. He comes out that way, take him down quick."

Eve charged in at the front of the building and, too impatient for the elevator, raced up the stairs. She found Dalrymple on four, weapon drawn as he waited beside the door.

"Lieutenant." He gave her a brief nod. "My partner's around the back. Subject's been inside less than five minutes. Backup's on the way."

"Good." She studied Dalrymple's face, found his eyes steady. "We won't wait for them. I go in low," she added, taking out her master and bypassing the locks.

"Fine with me." He was ready beside her.

"On three. One, two." They hit the door, went through high and low, back to back, sweeping with their weapons. Music was playing, a primitive backbeat of drums behind screaming guitars. In the tidy living area, the mood screen had been set on deep reds and swimming blues melting into each other.

She signaled Dalrymple to the left, had taken two steps to the right herself when a naked man came out of the kitchen area carrying a bottle of wine and a single red rose.

He screamed and dropped the bottle. Wine glugged out onto the rug. Holding the rose to his balls, he crouched. "Don't shoot! Jesus, don't shoot. Take anything you want. Anything. It's not even mine."

"NYPSD," Eve snapped at him. "On the floor, facedown, hands behind your head. Now!"

"Yes, ma'am, yes, ma'am." He all but dove to the rug. "I didn't do anything." He flinched when Eve dragged his hands down and cuffed them. "I was just going to meet Sunny. She said it would be okay."

"Who the hell are you?"

"Jimmy. Jimmy Ripsky. I go to college with Sunny. We're on winter break. She said her parents were out of town for a few days and we could use the place."

Eve holstered her weapon in disgust. The boy was shaking like a leaf. "Get him a blanket or something, Dalrymple. This isn't our man." She dragged him to his feet and had enough pity in her to uncuff him before gesturing to a chair. "Let's hear the whole story, Jimmy."

"That's it. Um" — cringing with embarrassment, he folded his arms over his crotch — "Sunny and I are, like, an item."

"And who's Sunny?"

"Sunny Polinsky. Sheila, I guess. Everybody calls her Sunny. This is her parents' place. Man, her father's going to kill me if he finds out."

"She called you?"

"Yeah. Well, no." He looked up with desperate gratitude when Dalrymple came in with a chenille throw. "I got an email from her this morning and a package. She said her parents were going south for the week and how I should come over tonight. About midnight, let myself in with the key she'd sent me. And I should, um, you know, get comfortable." He tucked the throw more securely around his legs. "She said she'd be here by twelve-thirty and I should, well, ah, be waiting in bed." He moistened his lips. "It was pretty, sort of, explicit for Sunny."

"Do you still have the email? The package the key came in?"

"I dumped the package in the recycler, but I've got the email. I printed it out. It's . . . it's a keeper, you know?"

"Right. Detective, call in your partner and my aide."

"Um, ma'am?" Jimmy began when Dalrymple turned away with his communicator.

"Dallas. Lieutenant."

"Yes, ma'am, Lieutenant. What's going on? Is Sunny okay?"

"She's fine. She's with her parents."

"But — she said she'd be here."

"I think someone else sent you that keeper email. Somebody who wanted me to have a little something extra to do tonight." But she sat, pulled out her palm-link. "I'm going to check out your story, Jimmy. If it all fits, Detective Dalrymple's going to arrange for a uniform to take you home. You can give him the printout of the email — and your computer."

"My computer? But —"

"It's police business," she said shortly. "You'll get it back."

"Well, that was fun," Peabody said when Eve resecured the door.

"A barrel of laughs."

"Poor kid. He was mortified. Here he was thinking he was going to have the sex of his dreams with his girl, and he gets busted."

"The fact that a rosebud managed to preserve most of his modesty tells me that the sex of his dreams outruns the reality." At Peabody's snort, Eve turned to the elevator. "Sunny backed up his story about them being an item. Not that I doubted it. The kid was too scared to lie. So . . . Dave's been keeping up with the social activities of his marks. He knows the family, the friends, and he knows how to use them."

She stepped out of the elevator, crossed the lobby. "For an MD in a maximum lockup, he managed to get his hands on plenty of data."

She paused at the door and simply stood for a moment looking out at the thin, steady snow. "You got off-planet clearance, Peabody?"

"Sure. It's a job requirement."

"Right. Well, go home and pack a bag. I want you on your way to Rexal on the first transport we can arrange. You and McNab can check out the facilities, find the unit Palmer had access to."

The initial rush from the idea of an off-planet assignment turned to ashes in her mouth. "McNab? I don't need McNab."

"When you find the unit, you'll need a good electronics man." Eve opened the door, and the blast of cold cooled the annoyed flush on Peabody's cheeks.

"He's a pain in the ass."

"Sure he is, but he knows his job. If Feeney can spare him, you're the off-planet team." She reached for her communicator, intending to interrupt Feeney's sleep and get the ball rolling. A scream from the end of the block had her drawing her weapon instead.

She pounded west, boots digging into the slick sidewalk. With one quick gesture, she signaled Dalrymple to stay at his post in the surveillance van.

She saw the woman first, wrapped in sleek black fur, clinging to a man with an overcoat over a tux. He was trying to shield her face and muffle her mouth against his shoulder. The pitch and volume of her screams indicated he wasn't doing a very good job of it.

"Police!". He shouted it as he saw Peabody and Eve running toward them. "Here's the police, honey. My God, my God, what's this city coming to? He threw it out, threw it out right at our feet."

It, Eve saw, was Carl Neissan. His naked and broken body lay face up against the curb. His head had been shaved, she noted, and the tender skin abraded and burned. His knees were shattered, his protruding tongue blackened. Around his neck, digging deep, was the signature noose. And the message carved into his chest was still red and raw.

WOE UNTO YOU ALSO, YE LAWYERS!

The woman's screaming had turned to wailing now. Eve tuned it out. With her eyes on the body, she pulled out her communicator. "This is Dallas, Lieutenant Eve. I have a homicide."

She gave Dispatch the necessary information, then turned to the male witness. "You live around here?"

"Yes, yes, this building on the corner. We were just coming home from a party when —"

"My aide is going to take your companion inside, away from this. Out of the cold. We'll need her statement. I'd appreciate it if you'd stay out here with me for a few minutes."

"Yes, of course. Yes. Honey." He tried to pry his wife's hands from around his neck. "Honey, you go with the policewoman. Go inside now."

"Peabody," Eve said under her breath, "take Honey out of here, get what you can out of her."

"Yes, sir. Ma'am, come with me." With a couple of firm tugs Peabody had the woman.

"It was such a shock," he continued. "She's very delicate, my wife. It's such a shock."

"Yes, sir, I'm sure it is. Can I have your names, please?"

"What? Oh. Fitzgerald. George and Maria."

Eve got the names and the address on record. In a few minutes she would have a crowd to deal with, she knew. Even jaded New Yorkers would gather around a dead, naked body on Madison Avenue.

"Can you — sir, look at me," she added when he continued to stare at the body. He was going faintly green. "Look at me," she repeated, "and try to tell me exactly what happened."

"It was all so fast, so shocking." Reaction began to set in, showing in the way his hand trembled as he pressed it to his face. "We'd just come from the Andersons'. They had a holiday party tonight. It's only a block over, so we walked. We'd just crossed the street when there was a squeal of brakes. I barely paid attention to it — you know how it is."

"Yes, sir. What did you see?"

"I glanced back, just out of reflex, I suppose. I saw a dark car — black, I think. No, no, not a car — one of those utility vehicles. The sporty ones. It stopped right here. Right here. You can still see the skid marks in the snow. And then the door opened. He pushed — he all but flung this poor man out, right at our feet."

"You saw the driver?"

"Yes, yes, quite clearly. This corner is very well lit. He was a young man, handsome. Light hair. He smiled . . . he smiled at me just as the door opened. Why, I think I smiled back. He had the kind of face that makes you smile. I'm sure I could identify him. I'm sure of it."

"Yeah." Eve let out a breath, watched the wind snatch it away as the first black-and-whites arrived on the scene. You wanted to be seen, didn't you, Dave? she thought. And you wanted me to be close, very close, when you gave me Carl.

"You can go inside with your wife, Mr Fitzgerald. I'll be in touch."

"Yes, of course. Thank you. I — it's Christmas week," he said with honest puzzlement in his eyes. "You live in the city, you know terrible things can and do happen. But it's Christmas week."

"Joy to the world," Eve murmured as he walked away. She turned around and ordered the uniforms to secure the scene and prepare for the crime-scene team. Then she crouched beside Carl and got to work.

CHAPTER
NINE

Eve spent most of the next thirty hours backtracking, searching for the step she was sure she had missed. With Peabody off-planet, she did the work herself, rerunning searches and scans, compiling data, studying reports.

She did personal drop-bys at both the safe house where Justine and her family were being kept and Mira's home. She ran checks on their security bracelets to confirm that they were in perfect working order.

He couldn't get to them, she assured herself as she paced her office. With them out of reach, he would have no choice but to come for her.

Jesus, she wanted him to come for her.

It was a mistake, she knew it was a mistake, to make it a personal battle. But she could see his face too clearly, hear his soft prep-school voice so perfectly.

But you see, Lieutenant Dallas, the work you do is nothing more than a stopgap. You don't change anything. However many criminals you lock up today, there'll be that many and more tomorrow. What I'm doing changes everything. The answers to questions every human being asks. How much is too much, how much will the mind accept, tolerate, bear, if you will, before it shuts down? And before it does, what thoughts, what impulses go through the mind as the body dies?

Death, Lieutenant, is the focus of your work and of mine. And while we both enjoy the brutality that goes with it, in the end I'll have my answers. You'll only have more questions.

She only had one question now, Eve thought. Where are you, Dave?

She turned back to her computer. "Engage, open file Palmer, H3492-G. Cross-reference all files and data pertaining to David Palmer. Run probability scan. What is the probability that Palmer, David, is now residing in New York City?"

Working . . . Using current data the probability is ninety-seven point six that subject Palmer now resides in New York City.

"What is the probability that subject Palmer resides in a private home?"

Working . . . probability ninety-five point eight that subject Palmer is residing in a private home at this time.

"Given the status of the three remaining targets of subject Palmer, which individual will he attempt to abduct next?"

Working . . . strongest probability is for target Dallas, Lieutenant Eve. Attempts on targets Polinsky and Mira are illogical given current status.

"That's what you're hoping for."

She turned her head. Roarke stood in the doorway between their offices, watching her. "That's what I'm counting on."

"Why aren't you wearing a tracer bracelet?"

"They don't have one that goes with my outfit." She straightened, turned to face him. "I know what I'm doing."

"Do you?" He crossed to her. "Or are you too close to this one? He's gotten to you, Eve. He's upset your sense of balance. It's become almost intimate between you."

"It's always intimate."

"Maybe." He brushed a thumb just above her left cheek-bone. Her eyes were shadowed, her face pale. She was, he knew, running on nerves and determination now. He'd seen it before. "In any case, you've interrupted his work. He has no one now."

"He won't wait long. I don't need the computer analysis to tell me that. We've got less than forty hours left in the year. I don't want to start the new one knowing he's out there. He won't want to start it without me."

"Neither do I."

"You won't have to." Because she sensed he needed it, she leaned into him, closed her mouth over his. "We've got a date."

"I'll hold you to it."

When she started to ease back, he slid his arms around her, brought her close. "I'm not quite done here," he murmured, and sent her blood swimming with a hard and hungry kiss.

For a moment that was all there was. The taste of him, the feel of him pressed against her, the need they created in each other time after time erupting inside her.

Giving herself to it, and to him, was as natural as breathing.

"Roarke, remember how on Christmas Eve we got naked and crazy?"

"Mmm." He moved his mouth to her ear, felt her tremble. "I believe I recall something of that."

"Well, prepare yourself for a review on New Year's Eve." She drew his head back, framing his face as she smiled at him. "I've decided it's one of our holiday traditions."

"I feel very warmly toward tradition."

"Yeah, and if I feel much warmer right now, I'm not going to get my job done, so . . ."

She jumped away from him when her 'link beeped and all but pounced on it. "Dallas."

"Lieutenant." Peabody's face swam on, swam off again, then came shakily back.

"Peabody, either your transmission's poor or you've grown a second nose."

"The equipment here's worse than what we deal with at Central." The audio came through with a snake hiss of static. "And I don't even want to talk about the food. When you're planning your next holiday vacation, steer clear of Rexal."

"And it was top of my list. What have you got for me?"

"I think we just caught a break. We've tracked down at least one unit Palmer had access to. It's in the chapel. He convinced the padre he'd found God and wanted to read Scripture and write an inspirational book on salvation."

"Glory hallelujah. Can McNab access his files?"

"He says he can. Shut up, McNab." Peabody turned her head. The fact that her face became a vivid orange could have been temper or space interference. "I'm giving this report. And I'm reporting, sir, that Detective McNab is still one big butt ache."

"So noted. What does he have so far?"

"He found the files on the book Palmer used to hose the preacher. And he *claims* he's working down the levels. Hey!"

The buzzing increased and the screen blurred with color, lines, figures. Eve pressed her fingers to her eyes and prayed for patience.

McNab's cheerful, attractive face came on. Eve noted that he wore six tiny silver hoops in one ear. So he hadn't decided to tone down his look for a visit to a rehabilitation center.

"Dallas. This guy knows his electronics, so he took basic precautions with his personal data, but — take a hike, She-Body, this is my area. Anyway, Lieutenant, I'm scraping off the excess now. He's got stuff tucked under his praise-the-Lord hype. It won't take me long to start picking it out. The trouble, other than your aide's constant griping, is transmitting to you. We've got crap equipment here and a meteor storm or some such happy shit happening. It's going to cause some problems."

"Can you work on the unit on a transport?"

"Ah . . . sure. Why not?"

"Confiscate the unit, catch the first transpo back. Report en route."

"Wow, that's iced. Confiscate. You hear that, She-Body? We're confiscating this little bastard."

"Get started," Eve ordered. "If they give you any grief, have the warden contact me. Dallas out."

Eve drove into Cop Central, making three unnecessary stops on the way. If Palmer was going to make a move on her, he'd do it on the street. He'd know he would never be able to break through the defenses of Roarke's fortress. But she spotted no tail, no shadow.

More, she didn't feel him.

Would he go for her in the station? she wondered as she took the glide up to the EDD sector to consult with Feeney. He'd used a cop's disguise to get to Carl. He could put it to use again, slip into the warrenlike building, blend with the uniforms.

It would be a risk, but a risk like that would increase the excitement, the satisfaction.

She studied faces as she went. Up glides, through breeze-ways, down corridors, past cubes and offices.

Once she'd updated Feeney and arranged for him to consult with McNab on the unit en route, she elbowed her way onto a packed elevator to make the trip to Commander Whitney's office.

She spent the morning moving through the building, inviting a confrontation, then she took to the streets for the afternoon.

She recanvased the houses she and Peabody had already hit. Left herself in the open. She bought bad coffee from a glide cart, loitered in the cold and the smoke of grilling soy-dogs.

What the hell was he waiting for? she thought in disgust, tossing the coffee cup into a recycling bin. The sound of a revving engine had her glancing over her shoulder. And she looked directly into Palmer's eyes.

He sat in his vehicle, grinned at her, blew her an exaggerated kiss. Even as she leaped forward, he hit vertical lift, shot up and streaked south.

She jumped into her car, going air as she squealed away from the curb. "Dispatch, Dallas, Lieutenant Eve. All units, all units in the vicinity of Park and Eighty respond. I'm in ground-to-air chase with murder suspect. Vehicle is a black new-issue Booster-6Z, New York license number Delta Able Zero-4821, temporary. Heading south on Park."

"Dispatch, Dallas. Received and confirmed. Units dispatched. Is subject vehicle in visual range?"

"No. Subject vehicle went air at Park and Eighty, headed south at high speed. Subject should be considered armed and dangerous."

"Acknowledged."

"Where'd you go, where'd you go, you little son of a bitch?" Eve rapped the wheel with her fist as she zipped down Park, shot down cross streets, circled back. "Too fast," she muttered. "You went under too fast. Your hole's got to be close."

She set down, did her best to bank her temper, to use her head and not her emotions. She'd let the search run another thirty minutes, though she'd already decided it was useless. He'd had the vehicle tucked away in a garage or lot minutes after she'd spotted him. After he'd made certain she'd spotted him.

That meant canvases of every parking facility in three sectors. Public and private. And with the budget, it would take days. The department wouldn't spare the manpower necessary to handle the job any quicker.

She stayed parked where she was, on the off chance that Palmer would try another taunt. After aborting the search, she did slow sweeps through the sectors herself, working off frustration before she drove home through the dark and the snarling traffic.

She didn't bother to snipe at Summerset, though he gave her ample opportunity. Instead, scooping up the cat, which was circling her legs, she climbed the stairs. Her intent was to take a blistering-hot shower, drink a gallon of coffee, and go back to work.

Her reality was to fall face down on the bed. Galahad climbed onto her butt, kneaded his way to comfort, curled up, and went on guard with his eyes slitted on the door.

That's how Roarke found them an hour later.

"I'll take over from here," he murmured, giving the cat a quick scratch between the ears. But when he started to drape a blanket over his wife, Eve stirred.

"I'm awake. I'm just —"

"Resting your eyes. Yes, I know." To keep her prone, Roarke stretched out beside her, stroked the hair away from her cheek. "Rest them a bit longer."

"I saw him today. The son of a bitch was ten feet away, and I lost him." She closed her eyes again. "He wants to piss me off so I stop thinking. Maybe I did, but I'm thinking now."

"And what are you thinking, Lieutenant?"

"That I've been counting too much on the fact that I know him, that I've been inside his head. I've been tracking him without factoring in one vital element."

"Which is?"

She opened her eyes again. "He's fucking crazy." She rolled over, stared at the sky window and the dark beyond it. "You can't predict insanity. Whatever the head shrinkers call it, it comes down to crazy. There's no physical, no psychological reason for it. It just is. He just is. I've been trying to predict the unpredictable. So I keep missing. It's not his work this time. It's payback. The other names on the list are incidental. It's me. He needed them to get to me."

"You'd already concluded that."

"Yeah, but what I didn't conclude, and what I'm concluding now, is he's willing to die, as long as he takes me out. He doesn't intend to go back to prison. I saw his eyes today. They were already dead."

"Which only makes him more dangerous."

"He has to find a way to get to me, so he'll take risks. But he won't risk going down before he's finished with me. He needs bait. Good bait. He must know about you."

She sat up now, raking her hair back. "I want you to wear a bracelet."

He lifted a brow. "I will if you will."

A muscle in her cheek jumped as she set her teeth. "I phrased that incorrectly. You're *going* to wear a bracelet."

"I believe such things are voluntary unless the subject has committed a crime." He sat up himself, caught her chin in his hand. "He won't get to you through me. That I can promise. But if you expect me to wear NYPSD accessories, you'll have to wear a matching one. Since you won't, I don't believe this conversation has a point."

"Goddamn it, Roarke. I can slap you into protective custody. I can order taps on all your communications, have you shadowed —"

"No," he interrupted, and infuriated her by kissing her lightly. "You can't. My lawyers will tap-dance all over your warrants. Stop." He tightened his grip on her chin before she could curse him again. And this time there was no light kiss, no flicker of amusement in his eyes. "You leave here every day to do a job that puts you in constant physical jeopardy. I don't ask you to change that. It's one of the reasons I fell in love with you. Who you are, what you do, why you do it. I don't ask you to change," he repeated. "Don't you ask me."

"It's just a precaution."

"No, it's a capitulation. If it was less, you'd be wearing one yourself."

She opened her mouth, shut it again, then shoved away and rose. "I hate when you're right. I really hate it. I'm going to take a shower. And don't even think about joining me and trying anything because I'm not too happy with you right now."

He merely reached out, snagged her hand, and yanked her back onto the bed. "I dare you to say that again in five minutes," he challenged and rolled on top of her.

She didn't say anything in five minutes, could barely speak in thirty. And when she did finally make it to the shower, her blood was still buzzing. She decided it was wiser not to comment when he joined her there. It would only appeal to his competitive streak.

She kept her silence and stepped out of the shower and into the drying tube. It gave her a very nice view. She let herself relax enough to enjoy it, watching the jets of water pulse and pound over Roarke as the hot air swirled around her.

She was back in the bedroom, just tugging on an ancient NYPSD sweatshirt and thinking about coffee and a long evening of work when her palm-link rang. Vaguely irritated with a call on her personal, she plucked it up from where she'd dumped it on the bedside table.

"Dallas."

"It was nice to see you today. In person. Face-to-face."

"Hello, Dave." With her free hand, she reached in her pocket, switched her communicator on, and plugged in Feeney's code. "Nice vehicle."

"Yes, I like it very much. Fast, efficient, spacious. You're looking a bit tired, Lieutenant. A bit pale. Overworked, as usual? Too bad you haven't been able to enjoy the holidays."

"They've had their moments."

"Mine have been very rewarding." His handsome face glowed with a smile. "It's so good to be back at work. Though I did manage to keep my hand in while I was away. But you and I — I'm sure we'll agree — know there's nothing like New York. Nothing like being home and doing what we love best."

"Too bad you won't be able to stay long."

"Oh, I intend to be here long enough to see the celebration in Times Square tomorrow night. To ring in the new year. In fact, I'm hoping we'll watch it together."

"Sorry, Dave. I have plans." From the corner of her eye, she watched Roarke come out of the bath. Watched him keep out of range, move directly to the bedroom computer, and begin to work manually.

"I think you'll change them. When you know who else I've invited to the party. I picked her up just a little while ago. You should be getting a call shortly from the guards you'd posted. The police haven't gotten any smarter since I've been gone." He let out a charming laugh. "I took a little video for you, Dallas. Take a look. I'll be in touch later to tell you what you need to do to keep her alive."

The image shifted. Eve's blood iced as she saw the woman in the cage. Unconscious, pale, one slim hand dangling through the bars.

"Transmitted from a public 'link," Roarke said from behind her. "Grand Central."

Dimly she heard Feeney giving her the same information through her communicator. Units were already on their way to the location.

He'd be gone. Of course they knew he'd already be gone.

"He has Mira." It was all she could say. "He has Mira."

CHAPTER
TEN

Panic wanted to win. It crawled in her belly, snaked up her throat. It made her hands shake until she balled them into fists.

It wanted to swallow her when she moved through Mira's house, when she found the broken security bracelet on the floor of the office.

"He used laser tools." Her voice was steady and cool as she bagged the bracelet. "He anticipated that she'd be wearing one and brought what was necessary to remove it."

"The MTs are taking the guards in. The two from outside were just stunned. But one of the inside team's in bad shape." Feeney crouched down next to her. "Looks like Palmer got in the back, bypassed the security system like a pro. He hit the one guard in the kitchen, used a stunner to take him out quick and quiet. From the looks of the living area, the second one gave him more trouble. They went a round in there. Mira must have been up here. If she had the door closed and was working, she wouldn't have heard anything. Room's fully soundproofed."

"So he takes out the security, four experienced cops, waltzes right in, dismantles her bracelet, and waltzes

104

out with her. We underestimated him, Feeney." And for that she would forever blame herself. "He's not what he was when I took him down before. He's studied up, he's learned, he's gotten himself into condition. He made good use of three years in a cage."

"She knows how his mind works." Feeney laid his hand on her shoulder. "Mira knows how to handle this kind of guy. She'll use that. She'll keep her cool and use it."

"No one knows how his mind works this time around. Thinking I did was part of the problem all along. I fucked up here, Feeney, and Mira's going to pay for it."

"You're wrong. The only fucking up you're doing is thinking that way now."

"I thought he might use Roarke as bait. Because if he's been studying me he knows that's where he could hit me the hardest." She made herself breathe slow as she got to her feet. "But he knows me better than I figured. He knows she matters to me."

"And he'll count on that messing you up. You gonna let it?"

"No." She breathed in again, exhaled. "No. I need McNab to shake something loose. What's their ETA?"

"Midday tomorrow. They had some transpo delays. The transmissions are full of blips, but I got that he's dug into some financials."

"Shoot whatever you've got to my home unit. I'll be working from there."

"We'll want to tap your palm-link."

"Yeah, he'll have figured that, but we'll do it anyway." She met Feeney's eyes. "We take the steps."

"We'll get her back, Dallas."

"Yeah, we will." She turned the sealed bracelet over in her hand. "If he hurts her, I'm taking him out." She lifted her gaze again. "Whatever line I have to cross, I take him out."

When she walked outside, Roarke was waiting. She hadn't argued when he'd come with her and could only be grateful that he was there to drive home so her mind could be free to think.

"Feeney's going to be sending me data," she began as she climbed into the car. "Financials. You'll be able to extrapolate faster. The sweepers will go through Mira's house, but he won't have left much, if anything. Anyway, it's not a question of IDing him. Peabody and McNab won't be back until midday tomorrow, so we'll be working with whatever they can send us while they're en route."

"I took a look at the alarms and security. It's a very good system. He used a sophisticated bypass unit to take it out without triggering the auto. It's not something your average citizen can access easily. I can help you trace the source."

"Doesn't matter at this point. Later we can deal with it. It's just another thread he left dangling, figuring I'd waste time pulling it and getting nowhere."

She rubbed at the headache behind her eyes. "I've got uniforms canvasing. One of the neighbors might have seen or heard something. It's useless, but it's routine and we might get lucky."

She closed her eyes, forced herself to think past the fear. "She's got until tomorrow, midnight. Dave wants some tradition and symbolism. He wants to welcome in the new year with me, and he needs her to get me there."

Her voice was too cool, Roarke thought. Too controlled. He'd seen the hint of panic in her eyes, and the grief. He let her hold in both as they arrived home, as she walked directly up to her office and called up all necessary files.

She added hard-copy data to the investigator's board she'd set up. And when she shifted Mira's photo from one area to the other, her fingers shook.

"Eve." He took her shoulders, turned her around. "Let it out."

"Can't. Don't talk to me."

"You can't work around it." He only tightened his grip when she tried to jerk away. "Let it out. Let it out," he said in a gentler tone. "I know what she means to you."

"God." She wrapped her arms around him, curling her hands up over his shoulders as she pressed her face into his neck. "Oh, God. Hold on. Just for a minute, hold on."

Her body shook, one hard wave of shudders after another. She didn't weep, but her breath hitched as he held her close. "I can't think about what he might do to her. If I think about it, I'll lose it."

"Then remember she's strong, and she's smart. She'll know what she has to do."

"Yeah." Her 'link signaled incoming data. "That'll be the financials."

"I'll start on them." He eased her back. "He won't win this round."

"Damn right."

She worked until her eyes and mind went blurry, then fueled up with coffee and worked some more. At just after two A.M. Feeney shot her more data. It told her that he, Peabody, and McNab were all still on the job.

"Basically," Roarke said, "this is just confirming what we already have. The accounts, the transfers. You need to find more. You need to look from a different angle." He glanced up to see Eve all but swaying on her feet. "And you need to sleep."

She would have argued, but it would have wasted time. "We both do. Just a little while. We can share the sleep chair. I want to stay close to this unit."

The caffeine in her system couldn't fight off exhaustion. Moments after closing her eyes, she fell into sleep. Where nightmares chased her.

Images of Mira trapped in a cage mixed and melded with memories of herself as a child, locked in a room. Horror, pain, fear lived in both places. He would come — Palmer, her father — he would come and he would hurt her because he could. Because he enjoyed it. Because she couldn't stop him.

Until she killed him.

But even then he came back and did it all again in her dreams.

She moaned in sleep, curled into Roarke.

It was the smell of coffee and food that woke her. She sat up with a jerk, blinked blindly in the dark, and found herself alone in the chair. She stumbled into the kitchen and saw Roarke already taking food from the AutoChef.

"You need to eat."

"Yeah, okay." But she went for the coffee first. "I was thinking about what you said, looking at a different angle." She sat, because he nudged her into a chair, and shoveled in food because it was in front of her. "What if he bought or rented this place he's got before he got to New York? A year ago, two years ago?"

"It's possible. I still haven't found any payments."

"Has to be there. Somewhere." She heard the ring of her palm-link from the other room and was on her feet. "Stay in here, do what you can to trace."

Deliberately she moved behind her desk, sat, composed her face. "Dallas."

"Good morning, Lieutenant. I hope you slept well."

"Like a top, Dave." She curled a hand under the desk.

"Good. I want you rested up for our date tonight. You've got, oh, let's see, just over sixteen and a half hours to get here. I have every confidence in you."

"You could tell me where you are, we can start our date early."

He laughed, obviously delighted with her. "And spoil the fun? I don't think so. We're puzzle solvers, Dallas. You find me by midnight and Dr Mira will remain perfectly safe. That's providing you come to see me alone. I'll know if you bring uninvited guests, as I have full security. Any gate-crashers, and the good doctor dies immediately and in great physical distress. I want to dance with you, Dallas. Just you. Understood?"

"It's always been you and me, Dave."

"Exactly. Come alone, by midnight, and we'll finish what we started three years ago."

"I don't know that she's still alive."

He only smiled. "You don't know that she's not." And broke transmission.

"Another public 'link," Roarke told her. "Port Authority."

"I need the location. If I'm not there by midnight, he'll kill her." She rose, paced. "He's got a place, one with full security. He's not bullshitting there. He'll have cameras, in and out. Sensors. He didn't have time to set all that up in a week, so either the place came equipped with them or he ordered them from prison courtesy of the chaplain."

"We can access tax records, blueprints, specs. It'll take time."

"Time's running out. Let's get started."

At two she received word that Peabody and McNab had landed, and she ordered them to bring the unit to her home office. He was close, she thought again, and none of them should waste time working downtown.

The minute they walked in, she began outlining her plan of attack. "McNab, set up over there. Start checking out any financials, transfers, transmissions, using the chaplain's name. Or a combo of his and Palmer's. Peabody, contact Whitney, request a canvas of all private garages in the suspect area. I want uniforms, every warm body we can find, hitting the public parking facilities with orders to confiscate and review all security tapes for the past week."

"All, Lieutenant?"

"Every last one."

She swung around and into Roarke's office. Using his auxiliary unit, she called up data, shot it to screen. "I've got the residences of Palmer's targets in blue," she told Roarke. "We run from mid to upper Manhattan, heaviest population on the East Side. We need to concentrate on private homes in this ten-block radius. Unless something jumps out at you, disregard anything that doesn't fit this profile."

She rolled her shoulders to relieve the tension, closed her eyes to clear her mind. "It'll have a basement. Probably two stories in addition to it. Fully soundproofed and most likely with its own vehicle storage area. I've got them looking at public storage, but I'm betting he has his own. He wants me to find him, goddamn it, so it can't be that hard. He wants me to work for it but not to fail. It's just personal for him, and without me . . ."

She trailed off, whirled around. "He needs me. Jesus. Check my name. Check deeds, mortgages, leases using my name."

"There's your new angle, Lieutenant," Roarke murmured as he set to work. "Very good."

"Toss it on screen," she asked even as she moved to stand behind him and watch. As her name popped up

111

with a list of liber and folio numbers she swore again. "How the hell did he get all that property?"

"That's not his, it's yours."

"What do you mean mine? I don't own anything."

"Properties I've transferred into your name." Roarke spoke absently as he continued the scan.

"Transferred? What the hell for?"

He skimmed a finger lightly over her wedding ring and earned a punch in the shoulder. "You're welcome."

"Take it back. All of it."

"It's complicated. Taxes. Really, you're doing me a favor. No, there's nothing here that isn't yours. We'll try a combination of names."

She wanted, badly, to seethe, but she didn't have time.

They found three listings for the name David Dallas in Manhattan.

"Get the property descriptions."

"I'm working on it. It takes a moment to hack into city hall."

Barely more than that for Roarke, Eve noted as the data flashed on screen. "No, that's downtown. Sex club. Try the next." She gripped the back of his chair, straining with impatience. "That's just out of the target area, but possible. Hold that and run the last. I'll be damned." She almost whispered it. "He reverted to type after all. That's his parents' house. He bought their place."

"Two and a half years ago," Roarke confirmed. "Using the name David Dallas. Your man was thinking ahead. Very far ahead. We'll find accounts in that name, or an account that he had and closed."

"Five blocks from here. The son of a bitch is five blocks from here." She leaned down, kissed the top of Roarke's head, and strode back into her office. "I've found it," she announced, then looked at her wrist unit. "We've got seven hours to figure out how to take him down."

She would go in alone. She insisted on it. She agreed to go in wired. Agreed to surveillance and backup at half-block intervals surrounding the house. For luck she pinned on the badge Peabody had given her, then waited with growing impatience as Feeney checked the transmitter.

"You're on," he told her. "Nothing I found on the video disc had equipment that can tag this pretty little bug. We've got a decoy so he'll think he's found one and deactivated it."

"Good thinking."

"You got to do it this way." He nodded at her. "I'd do the same. But you better understand I hear anything I don't like, I'm coming in. Roarke." He stepped back as Roarke came into the room. "I'll give you a minute here."

Roarke crossed to her, tapped a finger on her badge. "Funny, you don't look like Gary Cooper."

"Who?"

He smiled. "*High Noon*, darling Eve, though the clock's turned around on this one. We have a date in a couple of hours."

"I remember. I've got a present coming. I can do this."

"Yes." He kissed her, softly. "I know. Give my best to Mira."

"You bet. The team's moving into place now. I have to go."

"I'll see you soon."

He waited until she was gone, then walked outside himself and climbed casually into Feeney's unit. "I'll be riding with you."

Feeney scratched his chin. "Dallas won't like it."

"That's a pity. I spent the last few hours studying the schematics for the security on the Palmer house. I can bypass it, by remote."

"Can you, now?" Feeney said mildly.

Roarke turned his head, gave Feeney a level look. "I shouldn't need more than twenty minutes clear to manage it."

Feeney pursed his lips and started down the drive. "I'll see what we can do about that."

She went in at ten. It was best, she'd decided, not to cut it too close to the deadline. The old brownstone was lovely, in perfect repair. The security cameras and sensors were discreetly worked into the trim so as not to detract from its dignity.

As she walked to the door she was certain Palmer was watching. And that he was pleased. She gave the overhead camera a brief glance, then bypassed the locks with her master.

She closed the door at her back, heard the locks snick automatically back into place. As they did, the foyer lights flashed on.

"Good evening, Dallas." Palmer's voice flowed out of the intercom. "I'm so pleased you could make it. I was just assuring Doctor Mira that you'd be here soon so we could begin our end-of-year celebration. She's fine, by the way. Now, if you'd just remove your weapon —"

"No." She said it casually as she moved forward. "I'm not stripping down for you, Dave, so you can take me out as I come down the stairs. Let's not insult each other."

He laughed. "Well, I suppose you're right. Keep it. Take it out. Engage it. It's fine. Just remember, Doctor Mira's fate is in your hands. Come join us, Lieutenant. Let's party."

She'd been in the house before, when she interviewed his parents. Even if the basic setup hadn't come back to her, she'd taken time to study the blueprints. Still, she didn't move too quickly, but scanned cautiously for booby traps on the way through the house.

She turned at the kitchen, opened the basement door. The sound of cheering blasted up at her. The lights were on bright. She could see streamers, balloons, festive decorations.

She took her weapon out and started down.

He had champagne chilling in a bucket, pretty canapés spread on silver trays on a table draped with a colorful cloth.

And he had Mira in a cage.

"Lieutenant Dallas." Mira said it calmly, though her mind was screaming. She'd been careful to call Eve by her title, to keep their relationship professional, distant.

"Doctor." Palmer clucked his tongue. "I told you I'd do the talking. Lieutenant, you see this control I'm holding. Just so we understand each other right away, if I press this button, a very strong current will pass through the metal of the doctor's temporary home. She'll be dead in seconds. Even with your weapon on full, I'll have time to engage it. Actually, my nervous system will react in such a way to the shock that my finger will twitch involuntarily, and the doctor, shall we say, is toasted."

"Okay, Dave, but I intend to verify that Doctor Mira is unharmed. Are you hurt, Doctor?"

"No." And she'd managed so far to hold back hysteria. "He hasn't hurt me. And I don't think he will. You won't hurt me, will you, David? You know I want to help you. I understand how difficult all this has been for you, not having anyone who appreciates what you've been working to achieve."

"She's really good, isn't she?" he said to Eve. "So soothing. Since I don't want to show her any disrespect — you'll note I didn't remove her clothing for our little experiment — maybe you should tell her to shut the fuck up. Would you mind, Dallas?"

"Dave and I need to handle this, Dr Mira." Eve moved closer. "Don't we, Dave? It's you and me."

"I've waited for this for so long. You can see I've gone to quite a bit of trouble." He gestured with his free hand. "Maybe you'd like a drink, an hors d'oeuvre. We have a celebration going on. The end of the old, the birth of the new. Oh, and before I jam that wire you're wearing, tell the backup team that if anyone attempts entry, you both die."

"I'm sure they heard you. And they already have orders to hold back. You said to come alone," she reminded him. "So I did. I always played it straight with you."

"That's right. We learned to trust each other."

"Why stop now? I've got a deal for you, Dave. A trade. Me for Mira. You let her out of there, you let her go, and I'll get in. You'll have what you want."

"Eve, don't —" Mira's composure started to slip.

"This is between me and Dave." She kept her eye on him, level and cool. "That's what you want, isn't it? To put me in a cage, the way I put you in one. You've been thinking about it for three years. You've been planning it, working for it, arranging it step by step. And you did a damn good job this time around. Let her go, Dave. She was just bait, you got me here by using her. Let her go and I'll put down my weapon. I'll get in, and you'll have the kind of subject you've always wanted."

She took another step toward him, watching his eyes now, watching them consider. Desire. "She's a shrink, and she's not in the kind of condition I'm in — mental or physical. She sits at a desk and pokes into other people's minds. You start on her, she'll go down fast, give you no satisfaction. Think how long I'll last. Not just hours, days. Maybe weeks if you can hold the outside team off that long. You know it's going to end here, for both of us."

"Yes, I'm prepared for that."

"But this way, you can get your payback and finish your work. Two for one. But you have to let her out."

Music crashed out of the entertainment unit. On screen the revelers in Times Square swarmed like feverish ants.

"Put down the weapon now."

"Tell me it's a deal." She held her breath, lifted her weapon, aimed it at the center of his body. "Tell me it's a deal or I take you down. She goes, but I live. And you lose all around. Take the deal, Dave. You'll never get a better one."

"I'll take the deal." All but quivering with excitement, he rubbed a hand over his mouth. "Put the weapon down. Put it down and move away from it."

"Bring the cage down first. Bring it down to the floor so I know you mean it."

"I can still kill her." But he reached out to the console, touched a switch. The cage began to sway and lower.

"I know it. You've got the power here. I've just got a job. I'm sworn to protect her. Unlock the cage."

"Put the weapon down!" He shouted it out now, raising his voice over the music and cheers. "You said you'd put it down, now do it!"

"Okay. We've got a deal." Sweat slid down her back as she bent to lay the weapon on the floor. "You don't kill for the hell of it. It's for science. Unlock the cage and let her go." Eve lifted her hands, palms out.

On a bright laugh, he grabbed up a stunner, jabbed the air with it. "Just in case. You stay where you are, Dallas."

Her heart began to beat again when he put the control down, hit the button to release the locks. "Sorry you have to leave the party, Doctor Mira. But I promised this dance to the lieutenant."

"I need to help her out." Eve crouched to take Mira's hand. "Her muscles are stiff. She wouldn't have lasted for you, Dave." She gave Mira's hand one hard squeeze. "Get in, get in now."

"As soon as she's clear." Eve remained crouched, pushed Mira aside. As she used her body as a shield, she had time to register a movement on the stairs, then her clinch piece was in her hand.

"I lied, Dave." She watched his eyes go round with shock, saw him grab for the control, lower the stunner. The crowd cheered wildly as her blast took him full in the chest.

His body jerked, a quick and obscene dance. He was right, she noted, about the finger twitch. It depressed convulsively on the control even as he fell onto the cage.

Sparks showered from it, from his quaking body as she dragged Mira clear and curled herself over her.

"Your jacket's caught fire, Lieutenant." With admirable calm, Roarke bent over and patted out the spark that burned the leather at her shoulder.

"What the hell are you doing here?"

"Just picking up my wife for our date." He reached down gently and helped Mira to her feet. "He's gone," Roarke murmured, and brushed tears from her cheeks.

"I couldn't reach him. I tried, for hours after I woke up in that . . . in that thing. But I couldn't reach him."

Mira turned to Eve. "You could, in the only way that was left. I was afraid you'd —" She broke off, shook her head. "I was afraid you'd come, and afraid you wouldn't. I should have trusted you to do what had to be done."

When she caught Eve in a hard embrace, pressed her cheek against hers, Eve held on, just held on, then eased away, awkwardly patting Mira's back. "It was a team effort — including this civilian this time around. Go spend New Year's with your family. We'll worry about the routine later."

"Thank you for my life." She kissed Eve's cheek, then turned and kissed Roarke's. And didn't begin to weep again until she was upstairs.

"Well, Lieutenant, it's a very fitting end."

She followed Roarke's gaze, studied Palmer, and felt nothing but quiet relief. "To the man or the year?"

"To both." He stepped to the champagne, sniffing it as he drew it from the bucket. "Your team's on the way in. But I think we could take time for a toast."

"Not here. Not with that." She took the bottle, dumped it back into the bucket. On impulse, she took the badge off her shirt, pinned it on his. "Routine can wait. I want to collect on my present."

"Where do you want to go?"

"Just home." She slid an arm around his waist, moving toward the stairs as cops started down. "Just home, with you." She heard the crowd erupt with another cheer. "Happy New Year."

"Not quite yet. But it will be."

120

INTERLUDE
IN DEATH

Learning is not child's play;
We cannot learn without pain.

ARISTOTLE

Happy is the child whose father goes to
the devil.

SIXTEENTH-CENTURY PROVERB

CHAPTER
ONE

The faces of murder were varied and complex. Some were as old as time and the furrows scoring them filled with the blood spilled by Cain. One brother's keeper was another's executioner.

Of course, it had been rather elementary to close that particular case. The list of suspects had been, after all, pretty limited.

But time had populated the earth until by the early spring of 2059 it so crawled with people that they spilled out from their native planet to jam man-made worlds and satellites. The skill and ability to create their own worlds, the sheer nerve to consider doing so, hadn't stopped them from killing their brothers.

The method was sometimes more subtle, often more vicious, but people being people could, just as easily, fall back on ramming a sharpened stick through another's heart over a nice patch of lettuce.

The centuries, and man's nature, had developed more than alternative ways to kill and a variety of victims and motives. They had created the need and the means to punish the guilty.

The punishing of the guilty and the demand for justice for the innocent became — perhaps had been since that first extreme case of sibling rivalry — an art and a science.

These days, murder got you more than a short trip to the Land of Nod. It shut you up in a steel and concrete cage where you'd have plenty of time to think about where you went wrong.

But getting the sinner where justice deemed he belonged was the trick. It required a system. And the system demanded its rules, techniques, manpower, organizations, and loopholes.

And the occasional seminar to educate and inform.

As far as Lieutenant Eve Dallas was concerned, she'd rather face a horde of torked-out chemi-heads than conduct a seminar on murder. At least the chemi-heads wouldn't embarrass you to death.

And as if it wasn't bad enough that she'd been drafted to attend the Interplanetary Law Enforcement and Security Conference, as if it wasn't horrifying enough that her own commander had ordered her to give a seminar, the whole ball of goddamn wax had to take shape off-planet.

Couldn't hold the sucker in New York, Eve thought as she lay face down on the hotel bed. Just couldn't find one spot on the whole fucking planet that could suit up. Nope, just had to send a bunch of cops and techs out into space.

God, she hated space travel.

And of all the places in the known universe, the site-selection committee had to dump them on the Olympus Resort. Not only was she a cop out of her element, but she was a cop out of her element giving a seminar in one of the conference rooms in one of the ridiculously plush hotels owned by her husband.

It was mortifying.

Sneaky son of a bitch, she thought, and wondered if any of the muscles and bones in her body that had dissolved during landing on Olympus had regenerated. He'd planned it, he'd worked it. And now she was paying for it.

She had to socialize, attend meetings. She had to — dear Christ — give a speech. And in less than a week, she would have to get back on that fancy flying death trap of Roarke's and face the journey home.

Since the idea of that made her stomach turn over, she considered the benefits of living out the rest of her life on Olympus.

How bad could it be?

The place had hotels and casinos and homes, bars, shops. Which meant it had people. When you had people, bless their mercenary hearts, you had crime. You had crime, you needed cops. She could trade in her New York Police and Security badge for an Interplanetary Law Enforcement shield.

"I could work for ILE," she muttered into the bed-spread.

"Certainly." On the other side of the room, Roarke finished studying a report on one of his other properties. "After a while, you wouldn't think twice about zipping from planet to space station to satellite. And you'd look charming in one of those blue-and-white uniforms and knee-high boots."

Her little fantasy fizzed. Interplanetary meant, after all, interplanetary. "Kiss my ass."

"All right." He walked over, bent down and laid his lips on her butt. Then began working his way up her back.

Unlike his wife, he was energized by space travel.

"If you think you're getting sex, pal, think again."

"I'm doing a lot of thinking." He indulged himself with the long, lean length of her. When he reached the nape of her neck, he rubbed his lips just below the ends of her short, disordered cap of hair. And feeling her quick shiver, grinned as he flipped her over.

Then he frowned a little, skimming a finger along the shallow dent in her chin. "You're a bit pale yet, aren't you?"

Her deep-golden-brown eyes stared sulkily into his. Her mouth, wide, mobile, twisted into a sneer. "When I'm on my feet again, I'm going to punch you in that pretty face of yours."

"I look forward to it. Meanwhile . . ." He reached down, began unbuttoning her shirt.

"Pervert."

"Thank you, Lieutenant." Because she was his, and it continuously delighted him, he brushed a kiss over her torso, then tugged off her boots, stripped off her trousers. "And I hope we'll get to the perversion part of our program shortly. But for now." He picked her up and carried her out of the bedroom. "I think we'll try a little postflight restorative."

"Why do I have to be naked?"

"I like you naked."

He stepped into a bathroom. No, not a bathroom, Eve mused. That was too ordinary a word for this oasis of sensual indulgence.

The tub was a lake, deep blue and fed by gleaming silver tubes twined together in flower shapes. Rose trees heavy with saucer-size white blooms flanked the marble stairs that led into a shower area where a waterfall already streamed gently down gleaming walls. The tall cylinders of mood and drying tubes were surrounded by spills of flowers and foliage, and she imagined that anyone using one of them would look like a statue in a garden.

A wall of glass offered a view of cloudless sky turned to gold by the tint of the privacy screen.

He set her down on the soft cushions of a sleep chair and walked to one of the curved counters that flowed around the walls. He slid open a panel in the tiles and set a program on the control pad hidden behind it.

Water began to spill into the tub, the lights dimmed, and music, softly sobbing strings, slid into the air.

"I'm taking a bath?" she asked him.

"Eventually. Relax. Close your eyes."

But she didn't close her eyes. It was too tempting just to watch him as he moved around the room, adding something frothy to the bath, pouring some pale gold liquid into a glass.

He was tall and had an innate sort of grace. Like a cat did, she thought. A big, dangerous cat that only pretended to be tame when it suited his mood. His hair was black and thick and longer than her own. It spilled nearly to his shoulders and provided a perfect frame for

129

a face that made her think of dark angels and doomed poets and ruthless warriors all at once.

When he looked at her with those hot and wildly blue eyes, the love inside her could spread so fast and strong, it hurt her heart to hold it.

He was hers, she thought. Ireland's former bad boy who had made his life, his fortune, his place by hook or — well — by crook.

"Drink this."

He liked to tend her, she mused as she took the glass he offered. She, lost child, hard-ass cop, could never figure out if it irritated or thrilled her. Mostly, she supposed, it just baffled her.

"What is it?"

"Good." He took it back from her, sipped himself to prove it.

When she sampled it, she found that he was right, as usual. He walked behind the chair, the amusement on his face plain when he tipped her back and her gaze narrowed with suspicion. "Close your eyes," he repeated and slipped goggles over her face. "One minute," he added.

Lights bled in front of her closed lids. Deep blues, warm reds in slow, melting patterns. She felt his hands, slicked with something cool and fragrant, knead her shoulders, the knotted muscles of her neck.

Her system, jangled from the flight, began to settle. "Well, this doesn't suck," she murmured, and let herself drift.

He took the glass from her hand as her body slipped into the ten-minute restorative program he'd selected. He'd told her one minute.

He'd lied.

When she was relaxed, he bent to kiss the top of her head, then draped a silk sheet over her. Nerves, he knew, had worn her out. Added to them the stress and fatigue of coming off a difficult case and being shot directly into an off-planet assignment that she detested, and it was no wonder her system was unsettled.

He left her sleeping and went out to see to a few minor details for the evening event. He'd just stepped back in when the timer of the program beeped softly and she stirred.

"Wow." She blinked, scooped at her hair when he set the goggles aside.

"Feel better?"

"Feel great."

"A little travel distress is easy enough to fix. The bath should finish it off."

She glanced over, saw that the tub was full, heaped with bubbles that swayed gently in the current of the jets. "I just bet it will." Smiling, she got up, crossed the room to step down into the sunken pool. And lowering herself neck-deep, she let out a long sigh.

"Can I have that wine or whatever the hell it is?"

"Sure." Obliging, he carried it over, set it on the wide lip behind her head.

"Thanks. I've gotta say, this is some . . ." She trailed off, pressed her fingers to her temple.

"Eve? Headache?" He reached out, concerned, and found himself flipping into the water with her.

When he surfaced, she was grinning, and her hand was cupped possessively between his legs. "Sucker," she said.

"Pervert."

"Oh, yeah. Let me show you how I finish off this little restorative program, ace."

Restored, and smug, she took a quick spin in the drying tube. If she was going to live only a few more days before crashing into a stray meteor and being burned to a cinder by exploding rocket fuel on the flight back home, she might as well make the best of it.

She snagged a robe, wrapped herself in it, and strolled back into the bedroom.

Roarke, already wearing trousers, was scanning what looked like encoded symbols as they scrolled across the screen of the bedroom tele-link. Her dress, at least she assumed it was a dress, was laid out on the bed.

She frowned at the sheer flow of bronze, walked over to finger the material. "Did I pack this?"

"No." He didn't bother to glance back, he could see her suspicious scowl clearly enough in his mind. "You packed several days' worth of shirts and trousers. Summerset made some adjustments in your conference wardrobe."

"Summerset." The name hissed like a snake between her lips. Roarke's major domo was a major pain in her ass. "You let him paw through my clothes? Now I have to burn them."

Though he'd made considerable adjustments to her wardrobe in the past year, there were, in his opinion, several items left that deserved burning. "He rarely paws. We're running a little behind," he added. "The cocktail reception started ten minutes ago."

"Just an excuse for a bunch of cops to get shit-faced. Don't see why I have to get dressed up for it."

"Image, darling Eve. You're a featured speaker and one of the event's VIPs."

"I hate that part. It's bad enough when I have to go to your deals."

"You shouldn't be nervous about your seminar."

"Who said I'm nervous?" She snatched up the dress. "Can you see through this thing?"

His lips quirked. "Not quite."

"Not quite" was accurate, she decided. The getup felt thin as a cloud, and that was good for comfort. The flimsy layers of it barely shielded the essentials. Still, as her fashion sense could be etched on a microchip with room to spare, she had to figure Roarke knew what he was doing.

At the sound of the mixed voices rolling out of the ballroom as they approached, Eve shook her head. "I bet half of them are already in the bag. You're serving prime stuff in there, aren't you?"

"Only the best for our hardworking civil servants." Knowing his woman, Roarke took her hand and pulled her through the open doorway.

The ballroom was huge, and packed. They'd come from all over the planet, and its satellites. Police officials, technicians, expert consultants. The brains and the brawn of law enforcement.

"Doesn't it make you nervous to be in the same room with, what, about four thousand cops?" she asked him.

"On the contrary, Lieutenant," he said laughingly. "I feel very safe."

"Some of these guys probably tried to put you away once upon a time."

"So did you." Now he took her hand and, before she could stop him, kissed it. "Look where it got you."

"Dallas!" Officer Delia Peabody, decked out in a short red dress instead of her standard starched uniform, rushed up. Her dark bowl of hair had been fluffed and curled. And, Eve noted, the tall glass in her hand was already half empty.

"Peabody. Looks like you got here."

"The transport was on time, no problem. Roarke, this place is seriously iced. I can't believe I'm here. I really appreciate you getting me in, Dallas."

She hadn't arranged it as a favor, exactly. If she was going to suffer through a seminar, Eve had figured her aide should suffer, too. But from the look of things Peabody seemed to be bearing up.

"I came in with Feeney and his wife," Peabody went on. "And Dr Mira and her husband. Morris and Dickhead and Silas from Security, Leward from Anti-Crime — they're all around somewhere. Some of the other guys from Central and the precincts. NYPSD is really well represented."

"Great." She could expect to get ragged on about her speech for weeks.

"We're going to have a little reunion later in the Moonscape Lounge."

"Reunion? We just saw each other yesterday."

"On-planet." Peabody's lips, slicked deep red, threatened to pout. "This is different."

Eve scowled at her aide's fancy party dress. "You're telling me."

"Why don't I get you ladies a drink? Wine, Eve? And Peabody?"

"I'm having an Awesome Orgasm. The drink, I mean, not, you know, personally."

Amused, Roarke brushed a hand over her shoulder. "I'll take care of it."

"Boy, could he ever," Peabody muttered as he walked away.

"Button it." Eve scanned the room, separating cops from spouses, from techs, from consultants. She focused in on a large group gathered in the southeast corner of the ball-room. "What's the deal there?"

"That's the big wheel. Former Commander Douglas R. Skinner." Peabody gestured with her glass, then took a long drink. "You ever meet him?"

"No. Heard about him plenty, though."

"He's a legend. I haven't gotten a look yet because there's been about a hundred people around him since I got here. I've read most of his books. The way he came through the Urban Wars, kept his own turf secure. He was wounded during the Atlanta Siege, but held the line. He's a real hero."

"Cops aren't heroes, Peabody. We just do the job."

CHAPTER
TWO

Eve wasn't interested in legends or heroes or retired cops who raked in enormous fees playing the lecture circuit or consulting. She was interested in finishing her one drink, putting in an appearance at the reception — and only because her own commander had ordered her to do so — then making herself scarce.

Tomorrow, she thought, was soon enough to get down to work. From the noise level of the crowd, everyone else thought so, too.

But it appeared the legend was interested in her.

She barely had the wineglass in her hand, was just calculating the least annoying route around the room, when someone tapped on her shoulder.

"Lieutenant Dallas." A thin man with dark hair cut so short it looked like sandpaper glued to his scalp, nodded at her. "Bryson Hayes, Commander Skinner's personal adjutant. The commander would very much like to meet you. If you'd come with me."

"The commander," she returned even as Hayes started to turn away, "looks pretty occupied at the moment. I'll be around all week."

After one slow blink, Hayes simply stared at her. "The commander would like to meet you now,

Lieutenant. His schedule through the conference is very demanding."

"Go on." Peabody whispered it as she nudged Eve with her elbow. "Go on, Dallas."

"We'd be delighted to meet with Commander Skinner." Roarke solved the problem by setting his own drink aside, then taking both Eve's and Peabody's arms. It earned him an adoring-puppy look from Peabody and a narrow scowl from his wife.

Before Hayes could object or adjust, Roarke led both women across the ballroom.

"You're just doing this to piss me off," Eve commented.

"Not entirely, but I did enjoy pissing Hayes off. Just a bit of politics, Lieutenant." He gave her arm a friendly squeeze. "It never hurts to play them."

He slipped through the crowd smoothly, and only smiled when Hayes, a muscle working in his jaw, caught up in time to break a path through the last knot of people.

Skinner was short. His reputation was so large, it surprised Eve to note that he barely reached her shoulders. She knew him to be seventy, but he'd kept himself in shape. His face was lined, but it didn't sag. Nor did his body. He'd allowed his hair to gray, but not to thin, and he wore it militarily trim. His eyes, under straight silver brows, were a hard marble blue.

He held a short glass, the amber liquid inside neat. The heavy gold of his fifty-year ring gleamed on his finger.

She took his measure in a matter of seconds as, she noted, he took hers.

"Lieutenant Dallas."

"Commander Skinner." She accepted the hand he held out, found it cool, dry and more frail than she'd expected. "My aide, Officer Peabody."

His gaze stayed on Eve's face an extra beat, then shifted to Peabody. His lips curved. "Officer, always a pleasure to meet one of our men or women in uniform."

"Thank you, sir. It's an honor to meet you, Commander. You're one of the reasons I joined the force."

"I'm sure the NYPSD is lucky to have you. Lieutenant, I'd —"

"My husband," Eve interrupted. "Roarke."

Skinner's expression didn't waver, but it chilled. "Yes, I recognized Roarke. I spent some of my last decade on the job studying you."

"I'm flattered. I believe this is your wife." Roarke turned his attention to the woman beside Skinner. "It's a pleasure to meet you."

"Thank you." Her voice was the soft cream of the southern United States. "Your Olympus is a spectacular accomplishment. I'm looking forward to seeing more of it while we're here."

"I'd be happy to arrange a tour, transportation."

"You're too kind." She brushed a hand lightly over her husband's arm.

She was a striking woman. She had to be close to her husband in age, Eve thought, as their long marriage was part of Skinner's pristine rep. But either superior DNA or an excellent face-and-body team had kept her beauty youthful. Her hair was richly black, and the gorgeous tone of her skin indicated mixed race. She wore a sleek silver gown and starry diamonds as if she'd been born to such things.

When she looked at Eve it was with polite interest. "My husband admires your work, Lieutenant Dallas, and he's very exacting in his admiration. Roarke, why don't we give these two cops a little time to talk shop?"

"Thank you, Belle. Excuse us, won't you, Officer?" Skinner gestured toward a table guarded by a trio of black-suited men. "Lieutenant? Indulge me." When they sat, the men moved one step back.

"Bodyguards at a cop convention?"

"Habit. I wager you have your weapon and shield in your evening bag."

She acknowledged this with a little nod. She would have preferred to wear them, but the dress didn't allow for her choice of accessories. "What's this about, Commander?"

"Belle was right. I admire your work. I was intrigued to find us on the same program. You don't generally accept speaking engagements."

"No. I like the streets."

"So did I. It's like a virus in the blood." He leaned back, nursed his drink. The faint tremor in his hand surprised her. "But working the streets doesn't mean being on them, necessarily. Someone has to command — from a desk, an office, a war room. A good cop, a smart cop, moves up the ranks. As you have, Lieutenant."

"A good cop, a smart cop, closes cases and locks up the bad guys."

He gave one short laugh. "You think that's enough for captain's bars, for a command star? No, the word 'naïve' never came up in any of the reports I've read on you."

"Why should you read reports on me?"

"I may be retired from active duty, but I'm still a consultant. I still have my finger in the pie." He leaned forward again. "You've managed to work and close some very high-profile cases in the murder book, Lieutenant. While I don't always approve of your methods, the results are unarguable. It's rare for me to judge a female officer worthy of command."

"Excuse me. Back up. Female?"

He lifted his hand in a gesture that told her he'd had this discussion before and was vaguely weary of it. "I believe men and women have different primary functions. Man is the warrior, the provider, the defender. Woman is the procreator, the nurturer. There are numerous scientific theories that agree, and certainly social and religious weight to add."

"Is that so?" Eve said softly.

"Frankly, I've never approved of women on the force, or in certain areas of the civilian workplace. They're often a distraction and rarely fully committed to the job. Marriage and family soon — as they should for women — take priority."

140

"Commander Skinner, under the circumstances, the most courteous thing I can think of to say is you're full of shit."

He laughed, loud and long. "You live up to your reputation, Lieutenant. Your data also indicate that you're smart and that your badge isn't something you just pick up off the dresser every morning. It's what you are. Or were, in any case. We have that in common. For fifty years I made a difference, and my house was clean. I did what had to be done, then I did what came next. I was full commander at the age of forty-four. Would you like to be able to say the same?"

She knew when she was being played, and kept her face and tone neutral. "I haven't thought about it."

"If that's true, you disappoint me. If that's true, start thinking. Do you know, Lieutenant, how much closer you would be right now to a captaincy if you hadn't made some ill-advised personal decisions?"

"Really?" Something began to burn inside her gut. "And how would you know the promotion potential of a homicide cop in New York?"

"I've made it my business to know." His free hand balled into a fist, tapped lightly, rhythmically on the tabletop. "I have one regret, one piece of unfinished business from my active duty. One target I could never keep in my sights long enough to bring down. Between us, we could. I'll get you those captain bars, Lieutenant. You get me Roarke."

She looked down at her wine, slowly ran a fingertip around the rim. "Commander, you gave half a century of your life to the job. You shed blood for it. That's the single reason I'm not going to punch you in the face for that insult."

"Think carefully," he said as Eve got to her feet. "Sentiment over duty is never a smart choice. I intend to bring him down. I won't hesitate to break you to do it."

Riding on fury, she leaned down very close, and whispered in his ear. "Try it. You'll find out I'm no fucking nurturer."

She stepped away, only to have one of the bodyguards move into her path. "The commander," he said, "isn't finished speaking with you."

"I'm finished speaking with the commander."

His gaze shifted from her face briefly, and he gave the faintest nod before he edged closer, clamped a hand on her arm. "You'll want to sit down, Lieutenant, and wait until you've been dismissed."

"Move your hand. Move it now, or I'm going to hurt you."

He only tightened his grip. "Take your seat and wait for leave to go. Or you're going to be hurt."

She glanced back at Skinner, then into the guard's face. "Guess again." She used a short-arm jab to break his nose, then a quick snap kick to knock back the guard beside him as he surged forward.

By the time she'd spun around, planted, she had her hand in her bag and on her weapon. "Keep your dogs on a leash," she said to Skinner.

She scanned the faces of cops who'd turned, who'd moved forward, to see if there was trouble coming from another direction. Deciding against it, she turned away and walked through the buzzing crowd.

She was nearly at the door when Roarke fell in step beside her, draped an arm around her shoulders. "You got blood on your dress, darling."

"Yeah?" Still steaming, she glanced down at the small splatter. "It's not mine."

"I noticed."

"I need to talk to you."

"Um-hmm. Why don't we go upstairs, see what the valet can do about that bloodstain? You can talk before we come down to have a drink with your friends from Central."

"Why the hell didn't you tell me you knew Skinner?"

Roarke keyed in the code for the private elevator to the owner's suite. "I don't know him."

"He sure as hell knows you."

"So I gathered." He waited until they were inside the car before he pressed a kiss to her temple. "Eve, over the course of things, I've had a great many cops looking in my direction."

"He's still looking."

"He's welcome to. I'm a legitimate businessman. Practically a pillar. Redeemed by the love of a good woman."

"Don't make me hit you, too." She strode out of the elevator, across the sumptuous living area of the suite, and directly outside onto the terrace so she could finish steaming in fresh air. "The son of a bitch. The son of a bitch wants me to help him bring you down."

"Rather rude," Roarke said mildly. "To broach the subject on such a short acquaintance, and at a cocktail reception. Why did he think you'd agree?"

"He dangled a captaincy in my face. Tells me he can get it for me, otherwise I'm in the back of the line because of my poor personal choices."

"Meaning me." Amusement fled. "Is that true? Are your chances for promotion bogged down because of us?"

"How the hell do I know?" Still flying on the insult, she rounded on him. "Do you think I care about that? You think making rank drives me?"

"No." He walked to her, ran his hands up and down her arms. "I know what drives you. The dead drive you." He leaned forward, rested his lips on her brow. "He miscalculated."

"It was a stupid and senseless thing for him to do. He barely bothered to circle around much before he hit me with it. Bad strategy," she continued, "poor approach. He wants your ass, Roarke, and bad enough to risk censure for attempted bribery if I report the conversation — and anyone believes it. Why is that?"

"I don't know." And what you didn't know, he thought, was always dangerous. "I'll look into it. In any case, you certainly livened up the reception."

"Normally I'd've been more subtle, just kneed that jerk in the balls for getting in my way. But Skinner had gone into this tango about how women shouldn't be on the job because they're nurturers. Tagging the balls just seemed too girly at the time."

He laughed, drew her closer. "I love you, Eve."

"Yeah, yeah." But she was smiling again when she wrapped her arms around him.

As a rule, being crowded ass to ass at a table in a club where the entertainment included music that threatened the eardrums wasn't Eve's idea of a good time.

But when she was working off a good mad, it paid to have friends around.

The table was jammed with New York's finest. Her butt was squeezed between Roarke's and Feeney's, the Electronic Detective Division captain. Feeney's usually hangdog face was slack with amazement as he stared up at the stage.

On the other side of Roarke, Dr Mira, elegant despite the surroundings, sipped a Brandy Alexander and watched the entertainment — a three-piece combo whose costumes were red-white-and-blue body paint doing wild, trash-rock riffs on American folk songs. Rounding out the table were Morris, the medical examiner, and Peabody.

"Wife shouldn't've gone to bed." Feeney shook his head. "You have to see it to believe it."

"Hell of a show," Morris agreed. His long, dark braid was threaded through with silver rope, and the lapels of his calf-length jacket sparkled with the same sheen.

For a dead doctor, Eve thought, he was a very snappy dresser.

"But Dallas here" — Morris winked at her — "was quite some warm-up act."

"Har har," Eve replied.

Morris smiled serenely. "'Hotshot lieutenant decks legend of police lore's bodyguards at law enforcement convention on luxury off-planet resort'. You've got to play that all the way out."

"Nice left jab," Feeney commented. "Good follow-through on the kick. Skinner's an asshole."

"Why do you say that, Feeney?" Peabody demanded. "He's an icon."

"Who said icons can't be assholes?" he tossed back. "Likes to make out like he put down the Urban Wars single-handed. Goes around talking about them like it was all about duty and romance and patriotism. What it was, was about survival. And it was ugly."

"It's typical for some who've been through combat to romanticize it," Mira put in.

"Nothing romantic about slitting throats or seeing Fifth Avenue littered with body parts."

"Well, that's cheerful." Morris pushed Feeney's fresh glass in front of him. "Have another beer, Captain."

"Cops don't crow about doing the job." Feeney glugged down his beer. "They just do it. I'da been closer, Dallas, I'da helped you take down those spine crackers of his."

Because the wine and his mood made her sentimental, she jabbed him affectionately with her elbow. "You bet your ass. We can go find them and beat them brainless. You know, round out the evening's entertainment."

Roarke laid a hand on her back as one of his security people came to the table and leaned down to whisper in his ear. Humor vanished from his face as he nodded.

"Someone beat you to it," he announced. "We have what's left of a body on the stairway between the eighteenth and nineteenth floors."

CHAPTER
THREE

Eve stood at the top of the stairwell. The once pristine white walls were splattered with blood and gray matter. A nasty trail of both smeared the stairs. The body was sprawled on them, faceup.

There was enough of his face and hair left for her to identify him as the man whose nose she'd broken a few hours before.

"Looks like somebody was a lot more pissed off than I was. Your man got any Seal-It?" she asked Roarke.

When Roarke passed her the small can of sealant, she coated her hands, her shoes. "I could use a recorder. Peabody, help hotel security keep the stairwells blocked off. Morris." She tossed him the can. "With me."

Roarke gave her his security guard's lapel recorder. Stepped forward. Eve simply put a hand on his chest. "No civilians — whether they own the hotel or not. Just wait. Why don't you clear Feeney to confiscate the security disks for this sector of the hotel? It'll save time."

She didn't wait for an answer, but headed down the steps to the body. Crouched. "Didn't do this with fists." She examined his face. One side was nearly caved in, the other largely untouched. "Left arm's crushed. Guy was left-handed. I made that at the reception. They probably went for the left side first. Disabled him."

"Agreed. Dallas?" Morris jerked his head in the direction of the seventeenth floor. A thick metal bat coated with gore rested on a tread farther down the stairs. "That would've done the trick. I can consult with the local ME on the autopsy, but prelim eyeballing tells me that's the weapon. Do you want me to dig up some evidence bags, a couple of field kits?"

She started to speak, then hissed out a breath. The smell of death was in her nostrils, and it was too familiar. "Not our territory. We've got to go through station police. Goddamn it."

"There are ways to get around that, with your man owning the place."

"Maybe." She poked a sealed finger in a blood pool, nudged something metal and silver. And she recognized the star worn on the epaulets of hotel security.

"Who would be stupid enough to beat a man to death in a hotel full of cops?" Morris wondered.

She shook her head, got to her feet. "Let's get the ball rolling on this." When she reached the top of the steps, she scanned the hallway. If she'd been in New York, she would now give the body a thorough examination, establish time of death, gather data and trace evidence from the scene. She'd call her crime scene unit, the sweepers, and send out a team to do door-to-doors.

But she wasn't in New York.

"Has your security notified station police?" she asked Roarke.

"They're on their way."

"Good. Fine. We'll keep the area secure and offer any and all assistance." Deliberately, she switched off her recorder. "I don't have any authority here. Technically, I shouldn't have entered the crime scene area. I had a previous altercation with the victim, and that makes it stickier."

"I own this hotel, and I hold primary interest in this station. I can request the assistance of any law enforcement agent."

"Yeah, so we've got that clear." She looked at him. "One of your security uniforms is missing a star. It's down there, covered with body fluid."

"If one of my people is responsible, you'll have my full cooperation in identifying and apprehending him."

She nodded again. "So we've got that clear, too. What's your security setup for this sector?"

"Full-range cameras — corridors, elevators, and stairwells. Full soundproofing. Feeney's getting the disks."

"He'll have to hand them to station police. When it's homicide, they have a maximum of seventy-two hours before they're obliged to turn the investigation over to ILE. Since ILE has people on-site, they'd be wise to turn it over now."

"Is that what you want?"

"It's not a matter of what I want. Look, it's not my case."

He took a handkerchief out of his pocket and wiped the blood smear from her hand. "Isn't it?"

Then he turned as the chief of police stepped off the elevator.

Eve hadn't been expecting a statuesque brunette in a tiny black dress with enough hair to stuff a mattress. As she clipped down the hall on towering high heels, Eve heard Morris's reverent opinion.

"Hubba-hubba."

"Jeez, try for dignity," Eve scolded.

The brunette stopped, took a quick scan. "Roarke," she said in a voice that evoked images of hot desert nights.

"Chief. Lieutenant Dallas, NYPSD. Dr Morris, NYC Medical Examiner."

"Yes. Darcia Angelo. Chief of Olympus Police. Excuse my appearance. I was at one of the welcome events. I'm told we have a possible homicide."

"Verified homicide," Eve told her. "Victim's male, Caucasian, thirty-five to forty. Bludgeoned. The weapon, a metal bat, was left on scene. Preliminary visual exam indicates he's been dead under two hours."

"There's been a prelim exam?" Darcia asked. Coldly.

"Yes."

"Well, we won't quibble about that. I'll verify personally before my team gets here."

"Messy down there." Coolly, Eve handed over the can of Seal-It.

"Thanks." Darcia stepped out of her evening shoes. Eve couldn't fault her for it. She did the same thing herself, when she remembered. When she'd finished, she handed the can back to Eve. Darcia took a small recorder out of her purse, clipped it where the fabric of her dress dipped to hug her breasts.

Morris let out a long sigh as she walked into the stairwell. "Where do you find them?" he asked Roarke. "And how can I get one of my very own?"

Before Eve could snarl at him, Feeney hurried down the hall. "Got a snag with the disks," he announced. "Stairway cams were overridden for a fifty-minute period. You got nothing but static there, and static for two sixty-second intervals on the twentieth-floor corridor. Somebody knew what they were doing," he added. "It's a complex system, with a fail-safe backup plan. It took a pro — with access."

"With that time frame there had to be at least two people involved," Eve stated. "Premeditated, not impulse, not crime of passion."

"You got an ID on the victim? I can run a background check."

"Police chief's on scene," Eve said flatly.

For a moment Feeney looked blank. "Oh, right. Forgot we weren't home, sweet home. The locals going to squeeze us out?"

"You weren't," Darcia said as she came out of the stairwell, "ever — in an official capacity — in."

"On the contrary," Roarke told her. "I requested the assistance of the lieutenant and her team."

Irritation flickered across Darcia's face, but she controlled it quickly. "As is your privilege. Lieutenant, may I have a moment of your time?" Without waiting for an answer, Darcia walked down the corridor.

"Arrogant, territorial, pushy." Eve glared at Roarke. "You sure can pick them."

He only smiled as his wife's retreating back. "Yes, I certainly can."

"Look, Angelo, you want to bust my balls over doing a visual, you're wasting your time and mine." Eve tugged her lapel recorder free, held it out. "I verified a homicide, at the request of the property owner. Then I stepped back. I don't want your job, and I don't want your case. I get my fill of walking through blood in New York."

Darcia flipped her mane of glossy black hair. "Four months ago I was busting illegal dealers in Colombia, risking my life on a daily basis and still barely able to pay the rent on a stinking little two-room apartment. In the current climate, cops are not appreciated in my country. I like my new job."

She opened her purse, dropped Eve's recorder inside. "Is that job in jeopardy if I refuse to hand over this case to my employer's wife?"

"Roarke doesn't fight my battles, and he doesn't fire people because they might not agree with me."

"Good." Darcia nodded. "I worked illegals, bunko, robbery. Twelve years. I'm a good cop. Homicide, however, is not my specialty. I don't enjoy sharing, but I'd appreciate any help you and your associates are willing to give in this matter."

"Fine. So what was this dance about?"

"Simply? So you and I would both be aware it *is* my case."

"You need to be aware that earlier tonight I punched the dead man in the face."

"Why?" Darcia asked suspiciously.

"He got in my way."

"I see. It'll be interesting to find out if you and I can close this matter without getting in each other's way."

Two hours later, for convenience's sake, the two arms of the investigation gathered in Roarke's on-site office.

"The victim is identified as Reginald Weeks, thirty-eight. Current residence is Atlanta, Georgia, Earth. Married, no children. Current employer, Douglas R. Skinner, Incorporated. Function personal security." Darcia finished, inclined her head at Eve.

"Crime scene examination of body shows massive trauma." Eve picked up the narrative. "Cause of death, most likely, fractured skull. The left side of the head and body were severely traumatized. Victim was left-handed, and this method of attack indicates foreknowledge. Security for the stairwell and the twentieth floor were tampered with prior to and during the act. A metal bat has been taken into evidence and is presumed to be the murder weapon. Also taken into evidence a silver-plated star stud, identified as part of the hotel security team's uniform. Chief Angelo?"

"Background data so far retrieved on Weeks show no criminal activity. He had held his current employment for two years. Prior that, he was employed by Right Arm, a firm that handles personal security and security consults for members of the Conservative Party. Prior

154

to that he was in the military, Border Patrol, for six years."

"This tells us he knows how to follow orders," Eve continued. "He stepped up in my face tonight because Skinner, or one of Skinner's arms, signaled him to do so. He laid hands on me for the same reason. He's trained, and if he was good enough to last six years in the Border Patrol and land a job in Right Arm, he's not the type of guy who would go into a soundproof stairwell with a stranger, even under duress. If he'd been attacked in the corridor, there'd be a sign of it. If they took him on the twentieth floor, what the hell was he doing on the twentieth floor? His room, his security briefing room, and Skinner's suite are all on twenty-six."

"Could've been meeting a woman." Feeney stretched out his legs. "Conventionitis."

"That's a point," Eve allowed. "All evidence points to this being a planned attack, but a woman could have been used as a lure. We need to verify or eliminate that. You want to track it down, Feeney?"

"Captain Feeney may assist my officers in that area of investigation." Darcia merely lifted her eyebrows when Eve turned to her. "If he is agreeable. As I hope he will be to continuing to work with the hotel security team."

"We're a real agreeable group," Eve said with a wide, wide smile.

"Excellent. Then you have no problem accompanying me to twenty-six to inform the victim's employer of his death."

"Not a one. Peabody. My aide goes with me," Eve said before Darcia could speak. "Non-negotiable. Peabody," Eve said again, gesturing as she walked out of the room and left Darcia assigning her officers to different tasks. "I want your recorder on when we talk to Skinner."

"Yes, sir."

"If I get hung up, I need you to wheedle an update out of the local ME. If you can't open him up, tag Morris and have him use the good buddy, same field approach."

"Yes, sir."

"I want to find the uniform that star came from. We need to check recyclers, the valet, outside cleaning sources. Get chummy with the home team. I want to know the minute the sweepers and crime scene units reports are in. I'm betting there's going to be traces of Seal-It on that bat, and nobody's blood but the victim's on the scene. Fucking ambush," she grumbled, and turned as Darcia came out.

Darcia said nothing until she'd called for the elevator and stepped inside. "Do you have a history with Douglas Skinner, Lieutenant?"

"No. Not until tonight."

"My information is that he specifically called you to his table to speak with you privately. You, apparently, had words of disagreement, and when the victim attempted to prevent you from leaving the table, you struck him. Would this be accurate?"

"It would."

"What were those words of disagreement between you and Douglas Skinner?"

"Am I a suspect in this case or a consultant?"

"You're a consultant, and as such I would appreciate any and all data."

"I'll think about it." Eve stepped out on twenty-six.

"If you have nothing to hide."

"I'm a cop," Eve reminded her. "That line doesn't work on me." She rang the bell, waited. She watched the security light blink to green, kept her face blank while she and her companions were scanned. Moments later, Skinner opened the door himself.

"Lieutenant. It's a bit late for paying calls."

"It's never too late for official calls. Chief Angelo, Douglas Skinner."

"Pardon the intrusion, Commander Skinner." Darcia's voice was low and respectful, her face quietly sober. "We have some unfortunate news. May we come in?"

"Of course." He stepped back. He was dressed in the long white robe provided by the hotel, and his face looked pale against it. The large living area was dimly lit and fragrant from the bouquets of roses. He ordered the lights up 10 percent, and gestured toward the sofa.

"Please, ladies, sit. Can I get you anything? Coffee, perhaps?"

"We're not here to chat. Where were you between twenty-two hundred and midnight?"

"I don't like your tone, Lieutenant."

"Please, excuse us." Darcia stepped in smoothly. "It's been a difficult night. If I could ask you to verify your whereabouts, as a formality?"

"My wife and I came up to our suite a bit after ten. We retired early, as I have a long, busy day scheduled tomorrow. What's happened?"

"Weeks got his brains bashed in," Eve said.

"Weeks? Reggie?" Skinner stared at Eve. Those hard blue eyes widened, darkened, and seemed to draw a cast of gray over his skin as shock shifted into fury. "Dead? The boy is dead? Have you determined Roarke's 'whereabouts'? Or would you go so far as to cover up murder to protect him? She attacked Weeks only hours ago." He pointed at Eve. "An unprovoked and vicious assault on one of mine because I questioned her about her alliance with a criminal. You're a disgrace to your badge."

"One of us is," Eve agreed as Skinner sank into a chair.

"Commander." Darcia stepped forward. "I know this is a shock for you. I want to assure you that the Olympus PD is actively pursuing all avenues of investigation."

For a moment he said nothing, and the only sound was his quick, labored breathing. "I don't know you, Chief Angelo, but I know who pays you. I have no confidence in your investigation as long as it's bankrolled by Roarke. Now, excuse me. I have nothing more to say at this time. I need to contact Reggie's wife and tell her she's a widow."

CHAPTER
FOUR

"Well, that went well." Eve rolled her shoulders as she headed back to the elevator.

"If one doesn't mind being accused of being a fool or a dirty cop."

Eve punched the elevator button. "Ever hear the one about sticks and stones in Colombia?"

"I don't like that one." Obviously stewing, Darcia strode onto the elevator. "And I don't like your Commander Skinner."

"Hey, he's not mine."

"He implies Roarke is my puppet master. Why does he assume that, and why does he believe Roarke is responsible for Weeks's death?"

The quiet, respectful woman was gone, and in her place was a tough-eyed cop with steel in her voice. Eve began to see how Darcia Angelo had risen through twelve years in Colombia.

"One reason is Weeks annoyed me, and since I'm just a procreating, nurturing female, it would be up to my warrior, defender, penis-owning husband to follow through."

"Ah." Darcia sucked in her cheeks. "This is an attitude I recognize. Still, splattering a man's brains is

159

considerable overcompensation for such a minor infraction. A very large leap of conclusion for the commander to make. There's more."

"Might be. I haven't worked it out yet. Meanwhile, Skinner seemed awfully alert for someone who'd already gone to bed. And while the lights in the living area were on low when we walked in, they were full on in the bedroom off to the right. He didn't close the door all the way when he came out."

"Yes, I noticed that."

"Suite's set up along the same basic floor plan as the one I'm in. Second bedroom off to the left. There was a light on in there, too. His wife had that door open a crack. She was listening."

"I didn't catch that," Darcia mused, then glanced back when Peabody muttered.

"She missed it, too," Eve said. "She hates that. And if Belle Skinner was eavesdropping from the second bedroom, she wasn't snuggled up with the commander in the master, was she? No connubial bliss, which is interesting. And no alibi."

"What motive would Skinner have for killing one of his own bodyguards?"

"Something to think about. I want to check some things out." She stopped the elevator so both Darcia and Peabody could exit. "I'll get back to you."

Being willing to fall into step with Darcia Angelo didn't mean she couldn't make some lateral moves of her own. If she was going to wade into a murder investigation off her own turf, without her usual system and when her badge was little more than a fashion accessory, she was going to make use of whatever tools were available.

There was one particular tool she knew to be very versatile and flexible.

She was married to him.

She found Roarke, as she'd expected to, at work on the bedroom computer. He'd removed his dinner jacket, rolled up his sleeves. There was a pot of coffee beside him.

"What have you got?" She picked up his cup, gulped down half his coffee.

"Nothing that links me or any of my business dealings with Skinner. I have some interests in Atlanta, naturally."

"Naturally."

"Communications, electronics, entertainment. Real estate, of course." He took the cup back from her, idly rubbed her ass with his free hand. "And during one lovely interlude previous to my association with you, a nicely profitable smuggling enterprise. Federal infractions —"

"Infractions," she repeated.

"One could say. Nothing that bumped up against state or local authorities."

"Then you're missing something, because it's personal with him. It doesn't make any sense otherwise. You're not a major bad guy."

"Now you've hurt my feelings."

"Why does he latch on to you?" she demanded, ignoring him. "Fifty years a cop, he'd have seen it all. And he'd have lost plenty. There are stone killers out there, pedophiles, sexual predators, cannibals, for Christ's sake. So why are you stuck in his craw? He's been retired from active, what, six years, and —"

"Seven."

"Seven, then. Seven years. And he approaches me with what could be considered a bribe or blackmail, depending on your point of view, to pressure me into rolling over on you. It was arrogant and ill-conceived."

She thought it through as she paced. "I don't think he expected it to work. I think he expected me to tell him to fuck off. That way he could roll us into a ball together and shoot two for one."

"He can't touch you — or me, for that matter."

"He can make things hot by implicating us in a homicide. And he's laying the groundwork. He pushes my buttons in a public venue, then gets one of his monkeys to get in my face. Altercation ensues. A couple hours later, monkey has his brains splattered all over the stairway of a Roarke Enterprises hotel — and what's this! Why it's a clue, Sherlock, and a dandy one, too. A star stud from one of Roarke Securities uniforms, floating in the victim's blood."

"Not particularly subtle."

"He doesn't have time to be subtle. He's in a hurry," she continued. "I don't know why, but he's rushing things. Shove circumstantial evidence down the throat of the local authorities and they've got to pursue the possibility that the irritated husband and suspected interplanetary hoodlum ordered one of his own monkeys to teach Skinner's a lesson."

"You touched my wife, now I have to kill you?" Roarke's shrug was elegant and careless. "Overdramatic, over-romanticized. Particularly since you punched him in the face before I could ride to the rescue."

"In his narrow little world, men are the hunters, the defenders. It plays when you look at it through his window. It's another miscalculation though, because it's not your style. You want the hell beat out of someone, you do it yourself."

He smiled at her fondly. "I like watching you do it even more, darling."

She spared him a look. "Standard testing on you, any profile would kick the theory out of the park. You're just not hardwired to pay somebody to kill, or to get your dick in a twist because somebody hassles me. We could have Mira run you through a Level One testing just to push that aside."

"No, thank you, darling. More coffee?"

She grunted, paced a bit more while he rose to go to the mini AutoChef for a fresh pot and cups. "It's a sloppy frame. Thing is, Skinner believes you're capable, and that if he dumps enough on the ILE if and when they take over he'll push you into an investigative process that will mess you up — and me by association."

"Lieutenant, the ILE has investigated me in the past. They don't worry me. What does is that if it goes that far, your reputation and career could take some bruises. I won't tolerate that. I think the commander and I should have a chat."

"And what do you think he's counting on?" she demanded.

"Why disappoint him?" Coffee cup in hand, he sat on the arm of his chair. "I've compiled personal and professional data on Skinner. Nothing seems particularly relevant to this, but I haven't studied his case files in depth. Yet."

Eve set down the coffee he'd just poured her with a little snap of china on wood. "Case files? You hacked into his case files? Are you a lunatic? He gets wind of that, you're up on charges and in lockup before your fancy lawyers can knot their fancy ties."

"He won't get wind of it."

"CompuGuard —" She broke off, scowled at the bedroom unit. CompuGuard monitored all e-transmissions and programming on-planet or off. Though she was aware Roarke had unregistered equipment at home, the hotel system was a different matter. "Are you telling me this unit's unregistered?"

"Absolutely not." His expression was innocent as a choirboy's. "It's duly registered and meets all legal requirements. Or did until a couple of hours ago."

"You can't filter out CompuGuard in a few hours."

Roarke sighed heavily, shook his head. "First you hurt my feelings, now you insult me. I don't know why I put up with this abuse."

Then he moved fast, grabbing her up, hauling her against him and crushing her mouth with a kiss so hot she wondered if her lips were smoking.

"Oh, yes." He released her, picked up his coffee again. "That's why."

"If that was supposed to distract me from the fact that you've illegally blocked CompuGuard and broken into official data, it was a damn good try. But the joke's on you. I was going to ask you to dig up the data."

"Were you really, Lieutenant? You never fail to surprise me."

"They beat him until his bones were dust." Her tone was flat, dull. All cop. "They erased half his face. And left the other half clean so I'd know as soon as I saw him. The minute he stepped in front of me tonight, he was dead. I was the goddamn murder weapon." She looked back at the computer. "So. Let's get to work."

They culled out cases during Skinner's last decade of active duty and cross-referenced with anything relating to them during the seven years of his retirement. It overlapped the time before Roarke had come to America from Ireland, but it seemed a logical place to start.

As the caseload was enormous, they split it. Eve worked on the bedroom unit, and Roarke set up in the second bedroom.

By three, Eve's temples were throbbing, her stomach raw from caffeine intake. And she'd developed a new and reluctant admiration for Commander Skinner.

"Damn good cop," she acknowledged. Thorough, focused, and up until his retirement, he had apparently dedicated himself, body and soul, to the job.

How had it felt to step away from all that? she wondered. It had been his choice, after all. At sixty-four, retirement was an option, not a requirement.

He could have easily put in another ten years on active. He might have risen to commissioner.

Instead, he'd put in his fifty and then used that as a springboard in a run for Congress. And had fallen hard on his face. A half century of public service hadn't been enough to offset views so narrow even the most dug-in of the Conservative Party had balked. Added to that, his platform had swung unevenly from side to side.

He was an unwavering supporter of the Gun Ban, something the Conservatives tried to overturn at every opportunity. Yet he beat the drum to reinstate the death penalty, which alienated the Liberals from mid-road to far left.

He wanted to dissolve legal and regulated prostitution and strike out all legal and tax benefits for cohabitating couples. He preached about the sanctity of marriage, as long as it was heterosexual, but disavowed the government stipend for professional mothers.

Motherhood, the gospel according to Skinner stated, was a God-given duty, and payment in its own right.

His mixed-voice and muddled campaign had gone down in flames. However much he'd rebounded financially via lectures, books, and consults, Eve imagined he still bore the burns of that failure.

Still, she couldn't see how Roarke tied into it.

Rubbing her forehead, she pushed away and got up to work out the kinks. Maybe she was overreacting. Did she want it to be personal for Skinner because he'd made it personal for her? Maybe Roarke was no more than a symbol for Skinner. Someone who had slipped and slid around the system that Skinner himself had dedicated his life to.

She checked her wrist unit. Maybe she'd catch some sleep, go back to it fresh in the morning. She would juggle the data first, though, so that when she looked at it again it would be in a new pattern. Whatever she was missing — and her gut still told her she was missing something — might float to the top.

"Computer, extrapolate any and all references to Roarke . . ." She yawned hugely, shook her head to clear it. "In any and all files, personal and professional, under Skinner, Commander Douglas."

Working . . .

"List references chronologically, first to last, um . . . give me official police records first, followed by personal files."

Understood. Working . . . No reference to Roarke under Skinner, Commander Douglas police records. Reference under Skinner, Captain Douglas only . . . Extrapolating personal files . . .

"Yeah, well, you keep saying that, but . . ." Eve whirled around, stared at the monitor. "Computer, stop. List any and all reference to Roarke under Skinner, Douglas, any rank."

Working . . . first listed reference in Skinner, Captain Douglas, case file C-439014, to Roarke, Patrick a/k/a O'Hara, Sean, a/k/a MacNeil, Thomas, date stamped March, twelve, twenty-thirty-six. Subject Roarke suspect in illegal weapons running, illegal entry into United States, grand theft auto and conspiracy to murder of police officers. Subject believed to have fled Atlanta area, and subsequently the country. Last known residence, Dublin, Ireland. Case file complete, investigative data available. Do you wish full case file?

"Yes. In hard copy."

Working . . .

Eve sat down again, slowly as the computer hummed. 2036, she thought. Twenty-three years ago. Roarke would have been what, twelve, thirteen?

It wasn't Roarke that was at the root of Skinner's obsession.

It was Roarke's father.

At his own unit, Roarke ran through layers of Skinner's Financials. Among the most clear-cut motives for murder were greed, revenge, jealousy, sex, fear of disgrace, and profit. So he'd follow the money first.

There was a possibility, he'd decided, that Skinner had invested in one of his companies — or a competitor's. Perhaps he'd lost a substantial amount of money. Men had hated men for less.

And financially Skinner had taken a beating during his run for Congress. It had left him nearly broke as well as humiliated.

"Roarke."

"Hmm." He held up a finger to hold Eve off as she came into the room. "Communications," he said. "I have an interest in the Atlanta media sources, and they were very unkind to Skinner during his congressional attempt. This would have weighed heavily against his chances of winning. Media Network Link is mine outright, and they were downright vicious. Accurate, but vicious. Added to that, he's invested fairly heavily in Corday Electronics, based in Atlanta. My own company has eroded their profits and customer base steadily for the last four years. I really should finish them off with a takeover," he added as an afterthought.

"Roarke."

"Yes?" He reached around absently to take her hand as he continued to scroll data.

"It goes deeper than politics and stock options. Twenty-three years ago illegal arms dealers set up a base in Atlanta, and Skinner headed up the special unit formed to take them down. They had a weasel on the inside, and solid information. But when they moved in, it was a trap. Weasels turn both ways, and we all know it."

She took a deep breath, hoping she was telling it the way it should be told. Love twisted her up as often, maybe more often, than it smoothed things out for her.

"Thirteen cops were killed," she continued, "six more wounded. They were outgunned, but despite it, Skinner broke the cartel's back. The cartel lost twenty-two men, mostly soldiers. And he bagged two of the top line that night. That led to two more arrests in the next twelve months. But he lost one. He was never able to get his hands on one."

"Darling, I might've been precocious, but at twelve I'd yet to run arms, unless you're counting a few hand-helds or homemade boomers sold in alleyways. And I hadn't ventured beyond Dublin City. As for weaseling, that's something I've never stooped to."

"No." She kept staring at his face. "Not you."

And watched his eyes change, darken and chill as it fell into place for him. "Well, then," he said, very softly. "Son of a bitch."

CHAPTER
FIVE

As a boy, Roarke had been the favored recipient of his father's fists and boots. He'd usually seen them coming, and had avoided them when possible, lived with them when it wasn't.

To his knowledge, this was the first time the old man had sucker punched him from the grave.

Still, he sat calmly enough, reading the hard copy of the reports Eve had brought him. He was a long way from the skinny, battered boy who had run the Dublin alleyways. Though he didn't care much for having to remind himself of it now.

"This double cross went down a couple of months before my father ended up in the gutter with a knife in his throat. Apparently someone beat Skinner to him. He has that particular unsolved murder noted in his file here. Perhaps he arranged it."

"I don't think so." She wasn't quite sure how to approach Roarke on the subject of his father and his boyhood. He tended to walk away from his past, whereas she — well, she tended to walk into the wall of her own past no matter how often, how deliberately, she changed directions.

171

"Why do you say that? Look, Eve, it isn't the same for me as it is for you. You needn't be careful. He doesn't haunt me. Tell me why if my father slipped through Skinner's fingers in Atlanta, Skinner wouldn't arrange to have his throat slit in Dublin City."

"First, he was a cop, not an assassin. There's no record in the file that he'd located his target in Dublin. There's correspondence with Interpol, with local Irish authorities. He was working on extradition procedures should his target show up on Irish soil, and would likely have gotten the paperwork and the warrant. That's what he'd have wanted," she continued, and rose to prowl the room. "He'd want the bastard back on his own turf, back where it went down and his men were killed. He'd want that face-to-face. He didn't get it."

She turned back. "If he'd gotten it, he could've closed the book, moved on. And he wouldn't be compelled to go after you. You're what's left of the single biggest personal and professional failure of his life. He lost his men, and the person responsible for their loss got away from him."

"Dead wouldn't be enough, without arrest, trial, and sentencing."

"No, it wouldn't. And here you are, rich, successful, famous — and married, for Christ's sake — to a cop. I don't need Mira to draw me a profile on this one. Skinner believes that perpetrators of certain crimes, including any crime that results in the death of a police official, should pay with their life. After due process. Your father skipped out on that one. You're here, you pay."

172

"Then he's doomed to disappointment. For a number of reasons. One, I'm a great deal smarter than my father was." He rose, went to her, skimmed a finger down the dent in her chin. "And my cop is better than Skinner ever hoped to be."

"I have to take him down. I have to fuck over fifty years of duty, and take him down."

"I know." And would suffer for it, Roarke thought, as Skinner never would. As Skinner could never understand. "We need to sleep," he said and pressed his lips to her brow.

She dreamed of Dallas, and the frigid, filthy room in Texas where her father had kept her. She dreamed of cold and hunger and unspeakable fear. The red light from the sex club across the street flashed into the room, over her face. And over his face as he struck her.

She dreamed of pain when she dreamed of her father. The tearing of her young flesh as he forced himself into her. The snapping of bone, her own high, thin scream when he broke her arm.

She dreamed of blood.

Like Roarke's, her father had died by a knife. But the one that had killed him had been gripped in her own eight-year-old hand.

In the big, soft bed in the plush suite, she whimpered like a child. Beside her, Roarke gathered her close and held her until the dream died.

She was up and dressed by six. The snappy jacket that had ended up in her suitcase fit well over her harness and weapon. The weight of them made her feel more at home.

She used the bedroom 'link to contact Peabody. At least she assumed the lump under the heap of covers was Peabody.

"Whaa?"

"Wake up," Eve ordered. "I want your report in fifteen minutes."

"Who?"

"Jesus, Peabody. Get up, get dressed. Get here."

"Why don't I order up some breakfast?" Roarke suggested when she broke transmission.

"Fine, make it for a crowd. I'm going to spread a little sunshine and wake everybody up." She hesitated. "I trust my people, Roarke, and I know how much I can tell them. I don't know Angelo."

He continued to read the morning stock reports on-screen. "She works for me."

"So, one way or the other, does every third person in the known universe. That tells me nothing."

"What was your impression of her?"

"Sharp, smart, solid. And ambitious."

"So was mine," he said easily. "Or she wouldn't be chief of police on Olympus. Tell her what she needs to know. My father's unfortunate history doesn't trouble me."

"Will you talk to Mira?" She kept her gaze level as he rose, turned toward her. "I want to call her in, I want a consult. Will you talk to her?"

"I don't need a therapist, Eve. I'm not the one with nightmares." He cursed softly, ran a hand through his hair when her face went blank and still. "Sorry. Bloody hell. But my point is we each handle things as we handle them."

"And you can push and nudge and find ways to smooth it over for me. But I can't do that for you."

The temper in her voice alleviated a large slice of his guilt over mentioning her nightmare. "Screen off," he ordered and crossed to her. Took her face in his hands. "Let me tell you what I once told Mira — not in a consult, not in a session. You saved me, Eve." He watched her blink in absolute shock. "What you are, what I feel for you, what we are together saved me." He kept his eyes on hers as he kissed her. "Call your people. I'll contact Darcia."

He was nearly out of the room before she found her voice. "Roarke?" She never seemed to find the words as he did, but these came easy. "We saved each other."

There was no way she could make the huge, elegant parlor feel like one of the conference rooms in Cop Central. Especially when her team was gorging on cream pastries, strawberries the size of golf balls, and a couple of pigs' worth of real bacon.

It just served to remind her how much she hated being off her own turf.

"Peabody, update."

Peabody had to jerk herself out of the image of the good angel on her shoulder, sitting with her hands properly folded, and the bad angel, who was stuffing another cream bun in her greedy mouth. "Ah, sir. Autopsy was completed last night. They let Morris assist. Cause of death multiple trauma, most specifically the skull fracture. A lot of the injuries were postmortem. He's booked on a panel this morning, and has some sort of dead doctors' seminar later today, but Morris will finesse copies of the reports for you. Early word is the tox screen was clear."

"Sweepers?" Eve demanded.

"Sweepers' reports weren't complete as of oh-six-hundred. However, what I dug up confirmed your beliefs. Seal-It traces on the bat, no blood or bodily fluid but the victim's found on scene. No uniform missing an epaulet star has been found to date. Angelo's team's doing the run on recylers, valets, outside cleaning companies. My information is the uniforms are coded with the individual's ID number. When we find the uniform, we'll be able to trace the owner."

"I want that uniform," Eve stated, and when she turned to Feeney, the bad angel won. Peabody took another pastry.

"Had to be an inside job on the security cameras," he said. "Nobody gets access to Control without retina and palm scans and code clearance. The bypass was complicated, and it was done slick. Twelve people were in the control sector during the prime period last night. I'm running them."

"All right. We look for any connection to Skinner, any work-related reprimands, any sudden financial increase. Look twice if any of them were on the job before going into private security." She took a disk off the table, passed it to Feeney. "Run them with the names on here."

"No problem, but I work better when I know why I'm working."

"Those are the names of cops who went down in the line of duty in Atlanta twenty-three years ago. It was Skinner's operation." She took a deep breath. "Roarke's father was his weasel, and he turned a double cross."

When Feeney only nodded, Eve let out a breath. "One of the names on there is Thomas Weeks, father to Reginald Weeks, our victim. My guess is if Skinner had one of his slain officer's kids on his payroll, he's got others."

"Follows if one was used to build a frame around Roarke, another would be," Feeney added.

She checked her wrist unit when the door buzzer sounded. "That'll be Angelo. I want you running those names, Feeney, so I'm not giving them to her. Yet. But I'm going to tell her, and you, the rest of it."

While Eve was opening the door for Darcia, Skinner opened his to Roarke.

"A moment of your time, Commander."

"I have little to spare."

"Then we won't waste it." Roarke stepped inside, lifted a brow at Hayes. The man stood just behind and to the right of Skinner, and had his hand inside his suit jacket. "If you thought I was a threat you should've had your man answer the door."

"You're no threat to me."

"Then why don't we have that moment in private?"

"Anything you say to me can be said in front of my personal assistant."

"Very well. It would've been tidier, and certainly more efficient, if you'd come after me directly instead of using Lieutenant Dallas and sacrificing one of your own men."

"So you admit you had him killed."

"I don't order death. We're alone, Skinner, and I'm sure you've had these rooms secured against recording devices and surveillance cameras. You want to take me on, then do it. But have the balls to leave my family out of it."

Skinner's lips peeled back over his teeth. "Your father was a dickless coward and a pathetic drunk."

"Duly noted." Roarke walked to a chair, sat. "There, you see. We already have a point of agreement on that particular matter. First let me clarify that by 'family', I meant my wife. Second, I must tell you you're being too kind regarding Patrick Roarke. He was a vicious, small-minded bully and a petty criminal with delusions of grandeur. I hated him with every breath I took. So you see, I resent, quite strongly resent, being expected to pay for his many sins. I've plenty of my own, so if you want to try to put my head on a platter, just pick one. We'll work from there."

"Do you think because you wear a ten-thousand-dollar suit I can't smell the gutter on you?" Color began to flood Skinner's face, but when Hayes stepped forward, Skinner gestured him back with one sharp cut of the hand. "You're the same as he was. Worse, because he didn't pretend to be anything other than the useless piece of garbage he was. Blood tells."

"It may have once."

"You've made a joke out of the law, and now you hide behind a woman and a badge she's shamed."

Slowly now, Roarke got to his feet. "You know nothing of her. She's a miracle that I can't and wouldn't explain to the likes of you. But I can promise you, I hide behind nothing. You stand there, with fresh blood on your hands, behind your shield of blind righteousness and your memories of old glory. Your mistake, Skinner, was in trusting a man like my father to hold a bargain. And mine, it seems, was thinking you'd deal with me. So here's a warning for you."

He broke off as Hayes shifted. Fast as a rattler, Roarke drew a hand laser out of his pocket. "Take your bloody hand out of your coat while you still have one."

"You've no right, no authority to carry and draw a weapon."

Roarke stared at Skinner's furious face, then grinned. "What weapon? On your belly, Hayes, hands behind your head. Do it!" he ordered when Hayes shot Skinner a look. "Even on low these things give a nasty little jolt." He lowered the sight to crotch level. "Especially when they hit certain sensitive areas of the anatomy."

Though his breathing was now labored, Skinner gestured toward Hayes.

"To the warning. You step back from my wife. Step well and cleanly back, or you'll find the taste of me isn't to your liking."

"Will you have me beat to death in a stairwell?"

"You're a tedious man, Skinner," Roarke said with a sigh as he backed to the door. "Flaming tedious. I'd tell your men to have a care how they strut around and finger their weapons. This is my place."

Despite its size, Eve found the living area of the suite as stifling as a closed box. If she were on a case like this in New York, she would be on the streets, cursing at traffic as she fought her way to the lab to harass the techs, letting her mind shuffle possibilities as she warred with Rapid Cabs on the way to the morgue or back into Central.

The sweepers would tremble when she called demanding a final report. And the asses she would kick on her way through the investigation would be familiar.

This time around, Darcia Angelo got to have all the fun.

"Peabody, go down and record Skinner's keynote, since he's playing the show must go on and giving it on schedule."

"Yes, sir."

The morose tone had Eve asking, "What?"

"I know why you're leaning toward him for this, Dallas. I can see the angles, but I just can't adjust the pattern for them. He's a legend. Some cops go wrong because the pressure breaks them inside, or because of the temptations or just because they were bent that way to begin with. He never went wrong. It's an awful big leap to see him tossing aside everything he's stood for and killing one of his own to frame Roarke for something that happened when Roarke was a kid."

"Come up with a different theory, I'll listen. If you can't do the job, Peabody, tell me now. You're on your own time here."

"I can do the job." Her voice was as stiff as her shoulders as she started for the door. "I haven't been on my own time since I met you."

Eve set her teeth as the door slammed, and was already formulating the dressing-down as she marched across the room. Mira stopped her with a word.

"Eve. Let her go. You have to appreciate her position. It's difficult being caught between two of her heroes."

"Oh, for Christ's sake."

"Sit, before you wear a rut in this lovely floor. You're in a difficult position as well. The man you love, the job that defines you, and another man who you believe has crossed an indelible line."

"I need you to tell me if he could have crossed that line. I know what my gut tells me, what the pattern of evidence indicates. It's not enough. I have data on him. Most of it's public domain, but not all." She waited a beat while Mira simply continued to study her, calm as a lake. "I'm not going to tell you how I accessed it."

"I'm not going to ask you. I already know quite a bit about Douglas Skinner. He is a man devoted to justice — his own vision of it, one who has dedicated his life to what the badge stands for, one who has risked his life to serve and protect. Very much like you."

"That doesn't feel like much of a compliment right now."

"There is a parting of the ways between you, a very elemental one. He's compelled, has always been compelled, to spread his vision of justice like some are compelled to spread their vision of faith. You, Eve, at your core, stand for the victim. He stands for his vision. Over time, that vision has narrowed. Some can become victims of their own image until they become the image."

"He's lost the cop inside the hype."

"Cleanly said. Peabody's view of him is held by a great many people, a great many in law enforcement. It's not such a leap, psychologically speaking, for me to see him as becoming so obsessed by a mistake — and the mistake was his own — that cost the lives of men in his command, that that failure becomes the hungry monkey on his back."

"The man who's dead wasn't street scum. He was a young employee, one with a clean record, with a wife. The son of one of Skinner's dead. That's the leap I'm having trouble with, Dr Mira. Was the monkey so hungry that Skinner could order the death of an innocent man just to feed it?"

"If he could justify it in his mind, yes. Ends and means. How worried are you about Roarke?"

"He doesn't want me to worry about him," Eve answered.

"I imagine he's much more comfortable when he can worry about you. His father was abusive to him."

"Yeah. He's told me pieces of it. The old man knocked hell out of him, drunk or sober." Eve dragged a hand through her hair, walked back toward the window. There was barely a hint of sky traffic.

How, she wondered, did people stand the quiet, the stillness?

"He had Roarke running cons, picking pockets, then he'd slap him around if he didn't bring home enough. I take it his father wasn't much good at the rackets because they lived in a slum."

"His mother?"

"I don't know. He says he doesn't know either. It doesn't seem to matter to him." She turned back, sat down across from Mira. "Can that be? Can it really not matter to him what his father did to him, or that his mother left him to that?"

"He knows his father started him on the path of, let's say circumventing the law. That he has a predisposition for violence. He learned how to channel it, as you did. He had a goal — to get out, to have means and power. He accomplished that. Then he found you. He understands where he came from, and I imagine it's part of his pride that he became the kind of man a woman like you would love. And, knowing his . . . profile," Mira said with a smile. "I imagine he's determined to protect you and your career in this matter, every bit as much as you're determined to protect him and his reputation."

"I don't see how . . ." Realization hit, and Eve was just getting to her feet when Roarke walked in the door.

"Goddamn it. Goddamn it, Roarke. You went after Skinner."

CHAPTER
SIX

"Good morning, Dr Mira." Roarke closed the door behind him, then walked over to take Mira's hand. The move was as smooth as his voice, and his voice smooth as cream. "Can I get you some more tea?"

"No." Her lips twitched as she struggled to control a chuckle. "Thanks, but I really have to be going. I'm leading a seminar right after the keynote session."

"Don't think you can use her as a shield. I told you to stay away from Skinner."

"That's the second time someone's accused me of hiding behind a woman today." Though his voice remained mild, Eve knew the edge was there. "It's getting annoying."

"You want annoying?" Eve began.

"You'll have to forgive her," Roarke said to Mira as he walked her to the door. "Eve tends to become overexcited when I disobey."

"She's worried about you," Mira said under her breath.

"Well, she'll have to get over it. Have a good session." He nudged Mira out the door, closed it. Locked it. Turned. The edge was visible now. "I don't need a fucking shield."

184

"That was a figure of speech, and don't change the subject. You went at Skinner after I told you to stay clear of him."

"I don't take orders from you, Eve. I'm not a lapdog."

"You're a civilian," she shot back.

"And you're a consultant on someone else's case, and your authority here, in my bloody world, is a courtesy."

She opened her mouth, closed it. Hissed. Then she turned on her heel, strode out through the terrace doors, and kicked the railing several times.

"Feel better now?"

"Yes. Because I imagined it was your stupid, rock-hard head." She didn't look back, but braced her hands on the railing and looked out over what was indeed one of Roarke's worlds.

It was lavish and extravagant. The slick spears of other hotels, the tempting spreads of casinos, theaters, the glitter of restaurants were all perfectly placed. There were fountains, the silver ribbons of people glides, and the lush spread of parks where trees and flowers grew in sumptuous profusion.

She heard the click of his lighter, caught the scent of his obscenely expensive tobacco. He rarely smoked these days, she thought.

"If you'd told me it was important for you to have a face-to-face with Skinner, I'd have gone with you."

"I'm aware of that."

"Oh, Christ. Men. Look, you don't need to hide behind me or anybody. You're a tough, badass son of a

185

bitch with a really big penis and balls of titanium steel. Okay?"

He cocked his head. "One minute. I'm imagining throwing you off the balcony. Yes." He nodded, took a long drag on the cigarette. "That's indeed better."

"If Skinner took a couple of pops at your ego, it's because he knew it was a good target. That's what cops do. Why don't you just tell me what happened?"

"He made it clear, while Hayes stood there with a hand inside his coat and on his weapon, that my father was garbage and by association so am I. And that it was long past time for my comeuppance, so to speak."

"Did he say anything that led to him ordering Weeks killed?"

"On the contrary, he twice pointed the finger at me. Full of barely restrained fury and seething emotion. You could almost believe he meant it. I don't think he's well," Roarke continued and crushed out his cigarette. "Temper put a very unhealthy color in his face, strained his breathing. I'll have to take a pass through his medical records."

"I want to take a pass at his wife. Angelo agreed, after some minor complaints, to set it up so we can double-team her later this afternoon. Meanwhile, Peabody's on Skinner, between us we'll track down the uniform, and Feeney's running names. Somebody on your security staff worked that bypass. We find out who, we link them back to Skinner and get them into interview, we change the complexion of this. Maybe put it away before ILE comes in."

She glanced back toward the suite as the 'link beeped. "Are we okay now?"

"We seem to be."

"Good. Maybe that's Angelo with the setup for Belle Skinner." She moved past Roarke to the 'link. Rather than Darcia's exotic face, Feeney's droopy one blipped on screen.

"Might have something for you here. Zita Vinter, hotel security. She was in Control between twenty-one-thirty and twenty-three hundred last night. Crossed her with your list. Popped to Vinter, Detective Carl, Atlanta cop under Skinner. Line of duty during the botched bust. Vinter's wife was pregnant with their second kid — a son, Marshall, born two months after his death. Older kid was five. Daughter, Zita."

"Bullseye. What sector is she in now?"

"She didn't come in today. Didn't call in either, according to her supervisor. Got her home address. Want me to ride with you?"

She started to agree, then looked back at Roarke. "No, I got it. See what else you can find on her, okay? Maybe you can tag Peabody when the keynote crap's over. She's good at digging background details. Owe you one, Feeney. Let me have the address."

After she'd ended transmission, Eve hooked her thumbs in her front pockets and looked at Roarke. "You wouldn't know where 22 Athena Boulevard might be, would you?"

"I might be able to find it, yes."

"I bet." She picked up her palm-link from the desk, stuck it in her pocket. "I'm not riding in a limo to go

187

interview a suspect. It's unprofessional. Bad enough I'm taking some civilian wearing a fancy suit with me."

"Then I'll just have to come up with some alternate transportation."

"While you're at it, dig up your file on Zita Vinter, security sector."

He drew out his palm PC as they started out. "Always a pleasure to work with you, Lieutenant."

"Yeah, yeah." She stepped into the private elevator while he ordered something called a GF2000 brought to a garage slot. "Technically, I should contact Angelo and update her."

"No reason you can't. Once we're on the way."

"No reason. Saves time this way."

"That's your story, darling, and we'll stick to it. Vinter, Zita," he began as she scowled at him. "Twenty-eight. Two years with Atlanta PSD, then into private security. She worked for one of my organizations in Atlanta. Clean work record. Promoted to A Level over two years ago. She put in for the position here six months ago. She's single, lives alone. Lists her mother as next of kin. Her employment jacket's clean."

"When did you contract for this convention deal?"

"Just over six months ago," he said as they stepped off into the garage. "It was one of the incentives to have several of the facilities complete."

"How much do you want to bet Skinner's kept in close contact with his dead detective's daughter over the years? Angelo finesses a warrant for Vinter's 'link records, we're going to find transmissions to and from Atlanta. And not just to her mother."

When he stopped, put his PC away, she stared. "What the hell is this?"

Roarke ran a hand over the sleek chrome tube of the jet-bike. "Alternate transportation."

It looked fast and it looked mean, a powerful silver bullet on two silver wheels. She continued to stare as Roarke offered her a crash helmet.

"Safety first."

"Get a grip on yourself. With all your toys I know damn well you've got something around here with four wheels and doors."

"This is more fun." He dropped the helmet onto her head. "And I'm forced to remind you that part of this little interlude was meant to be a bit of a holiday for us."

He took a second helmet, put it on. Then tidily fastened hers. "This way you can be my biker bitch." When she showed her teeth, he only laughed and swung a leg nimbly over the tube. "And I mean that in the most flattering way possible."

"Why don't I pilot, and you can be my biker bitch?"

"Maybe later."

Swearing, she slid onto the bike behind him. He glanced back at her as she adjusted her seat, cupped her hands loosely at his hips. "Hang on," he told her.

He shot like a rocket out of the garage, and her arms latched like chains around his waist. "Lunatic!" she shouted as he blasted into traffic. Her heart flipped into her throat and stayed there while he swerved, threaded, streaked.

It wasn't that she minded speed. She liked to go fast, when she was manning the controls. There was a blur of color as they careened around an island of exotic wild-flowers. A stream of motion when they rushed by a people glide loaded with vacationers. Grimly determined to face her death without blinking, she stared at the snag of vehicular traffic dead ahead.

Felt the boost of thrusters between her legs. "Don't you —"

She could only yip and try not to choke on her own tongue as he took the jet-bike into a sharp climb. Wind screamed by her ears as they punched through the air.

"Shortcut," he shouted back to her, and there was laughter in his voice as he brought the bike down to the road again, smooth as icing on cake.

He braked in front of a blindingly white building, shut off all engines. "Well, then, it doesn't come up to sex, but it's definitely in the top ten in the grand scheme."

He swung off, removed his helmet.

"Do you know how many traffic violations you racked up in the last four minutes?"

"Who's counting?" He pulled off her helmet, then leaned down to bite her bottom lip.

"Eighteen," she informed him, pulling out her palm 'link to contact Darcia Angelo. She scanned the building as she relayed a message to Darcia's voicemail. Clean, almost brutally clean. Well constructed, from the look of it, tasteful and likely expensive.

"What do you pay your security people?"

"A Level?" They crossed the wide sidewalk to the building's front entrance. "About twice what a New York police lieutenant brings in annually, with a full benefit package, of course."

"What a racket." She waited while they were scanned at the door and Roarke coded in his master. The requisite computer voice welcomed him and wished him a safe and healthy day.

The lobby was tidy and quiet, really an extended foyer with straight lines and no fuss. At the visitors' panel, Eve identified herself and requested Zita Vinter.

I'm sorry, Dallas, Lieutenant Eve, Ms Vinter does not respond. Would you care to leave a message at this time?

"No, I don't care to leave a message at this time. This is police business. Clear me into Apartment Six-B."

I'm sorry, Dallas, Lieutenant Eve, your credentials are not recognized on this station and do not allow this system to bypass standard privacy and security regulations.

"How would you like me to bypass your circuits and stuff your motherboard up your —"

Warning! Verbal threats toward this system may result in arrest, prosecution, and monetary fines up to five thousand credits.

Before Eve could spit out a response, Roarke clamped a hand on her shoulder. "This is Roarke." He laid his hand on the palm plate. "ID 151, Level A.

You're ordered to clear me and Lieutenant Dallas to all areas of this compound."

Identification verified. Roarke and companion, Dallas, Eve, are cleared.

"Lieutenant," Eve said between her teeth as Roarke pulled her toward an elevator.

"Don't take it personally. Level six," he ordered.

"Damn machine treated me like a civilian." The insult of it was almost beyond her comprehension. "A *civilian*."

"Irritating, isn't it?" He strolled off onto the sixth floor.

"You enjoyed that, didn't you? That 'Roarke and companion' shit."

"I did, yes. Immensely." He gestured. "Six-B." When she said nothing, he rang the buzzer himself.

"She didn't answer before, she's not going to answer now."

"No." He dipped his hands lightly in his pockets. "Technically . . . I suppose you need to ask Chief Angelo to request a warrant for entry."

"Technically," Eve agreed.

"I am, however, the owner of this building, and the woman's employer."

"Doesn't give you any right to enter her apartment without legal authority or permission."

He simply stood, smiled, waited.

"Do it," Eve told him.

"Welcome to my world." Roarke keyed in his master code, then hummed when the lock light above the door remained red. "Well, well, she appears to have added a few touches of her own, blocked the master code. I'm afraid that's a violation of her lease agreement."

Eve felt the little twist in her gut and slipped her hand under her jacket to her weapon. "Get in."

Neither questioned that whatever methods had been taken, he could get around them. Through them. He took a small case of tools out of his pocket and removed the anti-intruder panel on the scanner and identification plate.

"Clever girl. She's added a number of tricky little paths here. This will take a minute."

Eve took out her 'link and called Peabody. "Track down Angelo," she ordered. "We're at 22 Athena Boulevard. Six-B. She needs to get over here. I want you with her."

"Yes, sir. What should I tell her?"

"To get here." She dropped the 'link back in her pocket, stepped back to Roarke just as the lock lights went green. "Move aside," she ordered and drew her weapon.

"I've been through a door with you before, Lieutenant." He took the hand laser out of his pocket, and ignored her snarl when she spotted it. "You prefer low, as I recall."

Since there wasn't any point in biting her tongue or slapping at him for carrying, she did neither. "On my count." She put a hand on the door, prepared to shove it open.

"Wait!" He caught the faint hum, and the sound sent his heart racing. The panel lights flashed red as he yanked Eve away from the door. They went down in a heap, his body covering hers.

She had that one breathless second to understand before the explosion blasted the door outward. A line of flame shot into the air, roaring across the hall where they'd been standing seconds before. Alarms screamed, and she felt the floor beneath her tremble at a second explosion, felt the blast of vicious heat all over her.

"Jesus! Jesus!" She struggled under him, slapped violently at the smoldering shoulder of his jacket with her bare hands. "You're on fire here."

Water spewed out of the ceiling as he sat up, stripped off the jacket. "Are you hurt?"

"No." She shook her head, shoved the hair soaked with the flood of the safety sprinklers out of her face. "Ears are ringing some. Where are you burned?" Her hands were racing over him as she pushed up to her knees.

"I'm not. The suit's fucked is all. Here, now. We're fine." He glanced back at the scarred and smoldering hole that had been the doorway. "But I'm afraid I'm going to have to evict Six-B."

Though she doubted it was necessary, Eve kept her weapon out as she picked her way over still-smoking chunks of wall and door. Smoke and wet clogged the air in the hall, in the apartment, but she could see at one glance that the explosion had been smaller than she'd assumed. And very contained.

"A little paint and you're back in business."

"The explosion was set to blow the door, and whoever was outside it." There were bits of broken crockery on the floor, and a vase of flowers had fallen over, spilling water into the rivers already formed by the sprinkler system.

The furniture was sodden, the walls smeared with streaks from smoke and soot. The hallway walls were a dead loss, but otherwise, the room was relatively undamaged.

Ignoring the shouts and voices from outside the apartment, he moved through it with Eve.

Zita was in bed, her arms crossed serenely across her chest. Holstering her weapon, Eve walked to the bed, used two fingers to check for the pulse in the woman's throat.

"She's dead."

CHAPTER
SEVEN

"Your definition of cooperation and teamwork apparently differs from mine, Lieutenant."

Wet, filthy, and riding on a vicious headache, Eve strained while Darcia completed her examination of the body. "I updated you."

"No, you left a terse message on my voicemail." Darcia straightened. With her sealed hands, she lifted the bottle of pills on the nightstand, bagged them. "When you were, apparently, at the point of illegally entering this unit."

"Property owner or his representative has the right to enter a private home if there is reasonable cause to believe a life or lives may be in danger, or that said property is threatened."

"Don't quote your regulations at me," Darcia snapped. "You cut me out."

Eve opened her mouth, then blew out a long breath. "Okay, I wouldn't say I cut you out, but I did an end run around you. In your place, I'd be just as pissed off. I'm used to being able to pursue a line on an investigation in my own way, on my own time."

"You are not primary on this case. I want this body bagged and removed," Darcia ordered the uniforms flanking the bedroom doors. "Probable cause of death, voluntary self-termination."

"Wait a minute, wait a minute. Wait!" Eve ordered, throwing out a hand to warn the uniforms back. "This isn't self-termination."

"I see an unmarked body, reclining in bed. Hair neatly brushed, cosmetic enhancements unblemished. I see on the bedside table a glass of white wine and a bottle of pills prescribed for use in painless, gentle self-termination. I have here," she continued, holding up another evidence bag containing a single sheet of paper, "a note clearly stating the subject's intention to end her own life due to her guilt about her part in the death of Reginald Weeks. A death she states was ordered by Roarke and for which she was paid fifty thousand, in cash. I see a satchel containing that precise amount of cash on the dresser."

"Roarke didn't order anyone's murder."

"Perhaps not. But I am accustomed to pursuing a line on an investigation in my own way. On my own time." She tossed Eve's words back at her. "Commander Skinner has lodged a complaint claiming that Roarke threatened him this morning, with words and a weapon. Security disks at the hotel verify that Roarke entered the commander's suite and remained there for seven minutes, forty-three seconds. This incident is corroborated by one Bryson Hayes, Skinner's personal assistant, who was present at the time."

There was no point in kicking something again and pretending it was Roarke's head. "Skinner's in this up to his armpits, and if you let him deflect your focus onto Roarke, you're not as smart as I thought. First things first. You're standing over a homicide, Chief Angelo. The second one Skinner's responsible for."

Darcia ordered her men away by pointing her finger. "Explain to me how this is homicide, and why I shouldn't have you taken to the first transport and removed from this station. Why I should not, on the evidence at hand, take Roarke in for interview as a suspect in the murder of Reginald Weeks." Temper pumped into her voice now, hot and sharp. "And let me make this clear: your husband's money pays my salary. It doesn't buy me."

Eve kept her focus on Darcia. "Peabody!" As she waited for her aide to come to the room, Eve struggled with her own temper.

"Sir?"

"What do you see?"

"Ah. Sir. Female, late twenties, medium build. No sign of struggle or distress." She broke off as Eve took an evidence bag from Darcia, passed it over. "Standard barb, commonly used in self-termination. Prescription calls for four units. All are missing. Date on the bottle is two weeks ago, prescribed and filled in Atlanta, Georgia."

Eve nodded when she saw the flicker in Darcia's eyes, then handed Peabody the note.

"Apparently suicide note, with signature. Computer-generated. The statement therein is contradictory to other evidence."

"Very good, Peabody. Tell Chief Angelo how it contradicts."

"Well, Lieutenant, most people don't have self-termination drugs tucked in their med cabinets. Unless you're suffering from an incurable and painful illness, it takes several tests and legalities to access the drug."

Darcia held up a hand. "All the more reason to have them around."

"No, sir."

"Ma'am," Darcia corrected with a smirk at Eve. "In my country a female superior is addressed as 'ma'am'."

"Yes, ma'am. It may be different in your country as to the process of accessing this sort of drug. In the States, you have to register. If you haven't — that is, if you're still alive within thirty days of filling the prescription, you're on auto-recall. The drugs are confiscated and you're required to submit to psychiatric testing and evaluation. But besides that, it doesn't play."

"Keep going, Peabody," Eve told her.

"The note claims she decided to off herself because she was guilty over events that took place last night. But she already had the drug in her possession. Why? And how? You established time of death at oh-four-hundred this morning, so she got her payoff and the guilts awful close, then the means to self-terminate just happen to be in her possession. It's way pat, if you follow me."

She paused, and when Darcia nodded a go-ahead, pulled in a breath and kept going. "Added to that, it doesn't follow that she would rig her apartment door to an explosive, or set another in the surveillance area to destroy the security disks of the building. Added to that," Peabody continued, obviously enjoying herself now, "Roarke's profile is directly opposed to hiring out hits, especially since Dallas popped the guy, which is one of the things he admires about her. So when you add that all up, it makes that note bogus, and this unattended death becomes a probable homicide."

"Peabody." Eve dabbed an imaginary tear from her eye. "You do me proud."

Darcia looked from one to the other. Her temper was still on the raw side, which she could admit colored her logic. Or had. "Perhaps, Officer Peabody, you could now explain how person or persons unknown gained access to this unit and persuaded this trained security expert to take termination drugs without her struggling."

"Well . . ."

"I'll take over now." Eve patted her shoulder. "You don't want to blow your streak. Person or persons unknown were admitted to the unit by the victim. Most likely to pay her off or to give her the next stage of instructions. The termination drugs were probably mixed into the wine. Person or persons unknown waited for her to slip into the first stage of the coma, at which time she was carried in here, laid out nice and pretty. The note was generated, the stage set. When it was determined that victim was dead, the explosives were rigged, and person or persons unknown went on their merry way."

"She sort of sees it," Peabody added helpfully. "Not like a psychic or anything. She just walks it through with the killer. Really mag."

"Okay, Peabody. She was a tool," Eve continued. "No more, no less. The same as Weeks was a tool. She probably joined the force to honor her father, and he used that, just as he's using Roarke's father to get to him. They don't mean anything to him as people, as flesh and blood. They're just steps and stages in his twenty-three-year war."

"Maybe not tools, then," Darcia countered, "but soldiers. To some generals they are just as dispensable. Excuse us, Officer Peabody, if you please."

"Yes, ma'am. Sir."

"I want an apology." She saw Eve wince, and smiled. "Yes, I know it'll hurt, so I want one. Not for pursuing a line of investigation, and so on. For not trusting me."

"I've known you less than twenty-four hours," Eve began, then winced again. "All right, shit. I apologize for not trusting you. And I'll go one better. For not respecting your authority."

"Accepted. I'm going to have the body taken to the ME, as a probable homicide. Your aide is very well trained."

"She's good," Eve agreed, since Peabody wasn't around to hear and get bigheaded about it. "And getting better."

"I missed the date, the significance, and I shouldn't have. I believe I would have seen these things once my annoyance with you had ebbed a bit, but that's beside the point. Now, I need to question Roarke regarding his conversation with the commander this morning, and regarding his association with Zita Vinter. To keep my official records clean, you are not included in this interview. I would appreciate it, however, if you'd remain and lead my team through the examination of the crime scene."

"No problem."

"I'll keep this as brief as I can, as I imagine both you and Roarke would like to go back and get out of those damp, dirty clothes." She tugged the sleeve of Eve's jacket as she passed. "That used to be very attractive."

"She was easier on me than I'd've been on her," Eve admitted as she rolled the stiffness out of her shoulders. She'd hit the floor under Roarke harder than she'd realized and figured she should take a look at the bruises.

After a long, hot shower.

Since Roarke's response to her statement was little more than a grunt as they rode up to their suite, she took his measure. He could use some cleaning up himself, she thought. He'd ditched the ruined jacket, and the shirt beneath it had taken a beating.

She wondered if her face was as dirty as his.

"As soon as we clean up," she began as she stepped out of the elevator and into the parlor. And that was as far as she got before she was pressed up against the elevator doors with his mouth ravaging hers.

Half her brain seemed to slide out through her ears. "Whoa. What?"

"Another few seconds." With his hands gripping her shoulders and his eyes hot he looked down at her. "We wouldn't be here."

"We are here."

"That's right." He jerked the jacket halfway down her arms, savaged her neck. "That's damn right. Now let's prove it." He stripped the jacket away, ripped her shirt at the shoulder. "I want my hands on you. Yours on me."

They already were. She tugged and tore at his ruined shirt, and because her hands were busy, used her teeth on him.

Less than a foot inside the room, they dragged each other to the floor. She rolled with him, fighting with the rest of his clothes, then arching like a bridge when his mouth clamped over her breast.

Need, deep and primal, gushed through her until she moaned his name. It was always his name. She wanted more. More to give, more to take. Her fingers dug into him — hard muscle, damp flesh. The scent of smoke and death smothered under the scent of him so that it filled her with the fevered mix of love and lust that he brought to her.

He couldn't get enough. It seemed he never could, or would. All of the hungers, the appetites and desires he'd known paled to nothing against the need he had for her — for everything she was. The strength of her, physical and that uniquely tensile morality, enraptured him. Challenged him.

To feel that strength tremble under him, open for him, merge with him, was the wonder of his life.

Her breathing was short, shallow, and he heard it catch, release on a strangled gasp when he drove her over the first peak. His own blood raged as he crushed his mouth to hers again, and plunged inside her.

All heat and speed and desperation. The sound of flesh slapping, sliding against flesh mixed with the sound of ragged breathing.

She heard him murmuring something — the language of his youth, so rarely used, slid exotically around her name. The pressure of pleasure built outrageously inside her, a glorious burn in the blood as he drove her past reason with deep, hard thrusts.

She clung, clung to the edge of it. Then his eyes were locked on hers, wild and blue. Love all but swamped her.

"Come with me." His voice was thick with Ireland. "Come with me now."

She held on, and on, watching those glorious eyes go blind. Held on, and on while his body plunged in hers. Then she let go, and went with him.

Sex, Eve had discovered, could, when it was done right, benefit body, mind, and spirit. She hardly bitched at all about having to dress up to meet with Belle Skinner at a ladies' tea. Her body felt loose and limber, and while the dress Roarke handed her didn't fit her image of cop, the weapon she snugged on under the long, fluid jacket made up for it.

"Are you intending to blast some of the other women over the watercress sandwiches and petit fours?" he asked.

"You never know." She looked at the gold earrings he held out, shrugged, then put them on. "While I'm swilling tea and browbeating Belle Skinner, you can follow up on a hunch for me. Do some digging, see if

Hayes was connected to any of the downed cops under Skinner's command during the botched bust. Something there too close for employer/employee relations."

"All right. Shoes."

She stared at the needle-thin heels and flimsy straps. "Is that what you call them? How come guys don't have to wear death traps like those?"

"I ask myself that same question every day." He took a long scan after she'd put them on. "Lieutenant, you look amazing."

"Feel like an idiot. How am I supposed to intimidate anyone dressed in this gear?"

"I'm sure you'll manage."

"Ladies' tea," she grumbled on the way out. "I don't know why Angelo can't just haul the woman in to her cop shop and deal."

"Don't forget your rubber hose and mini-stunner."

She smirked over her shoulder as she stepped onto the elevator. "Bite me."

"Already did."

The tea was already under way when Eve walked in. Women in flowy dresses, and some — Jesus — in hats, milled about and gathered under arbors of pink roses or spilled out onto a terrace where a harpist plucked strings and sang in a quavery voice that instantly irritated Eve's nerves.

Tiny crustless sandwiches and pink frosted cakes were arranged on clear glass platters. Shining silver pots steamed with tea that smelled, to Eve, entirely too much like the roses.

At such times she wondered how women weren't mortified to be women.

She tracked down Peabody first and was more than slightly amazed to see her stalwart aide decked out in a swirly flowered dress and a broad-brimmed straw hat with trailing ribbons.

"Jeez, Peabody, you look like a — what is it — milkmaid or something."

"Thanks, Dallas. Great shoes."

"Shut up. Run down Mira. I want her take on Skinner's wife. The two of you hang close while Angelo and I talk to her."

"Mrs Skinner's out on the terrace. Angelo just walked in. Wow, she's got some great DNA."

Eve glanced back, nodded to Angelo. The chief had chosen to wear cool white, but rather than flowing, the dress clung to every curve.

"On the terrace," Eve told her. "How do you want to play it?"

"Subtly, Lieutenant. Subtle's my style."

Eve lifted her brows. "I don't think so."

"Interview style," Darcia said and breezed onto the terrace. She stopped, poured tea, then strolled to the table where Belle was holding court. "Lovely party, Mrs Skinner. I know we all want to thank you for hosting this event. Such a nice break from the seminars and panels."

"It's important to remember that we're women, not just wives, mothers, career professionals."

"Absolutely. I wonder if Lieutenant Dallas and I might have a private word with you? We won't take up much of your time."

She laid a hand on the shoulder of one of the women seated at the table. Subtle, Eve thought. And effective, as the woman rose to give Darcia her chair.

"I must tell you how much I enjoyed the commander's keynote this morning," Darcia began. "So inspiring. It must be very difficult for him, and you, to deal with the convention after your tragic loss."

"Douglas and I both believe strongly in fulfilling our duties and responsibilities, whatever our personal troubles. Poor Reggie." She pressed her lips together. "It's horrible. Even being a cop's wife for half a century . . . you never get used to the shock of violent death."

"How well did you know Weeks?" Eve asked.

"Loss and shock and sorrow aren't connected only to personal knowledge, Lieutenant." Belle's voice went cool. "But I knew him quite well, actually. Douglas and I believe in forming strong and caring relationships with our employees."

Likes Angelo, Eve thought. Hates me. Okay, then. "I guess being full of shock and sorrow is the reason you eavesdropped from your bedroom instead of coming out when we notified Commander Skinner that one of his security team had been murdered."

Belle's face went very blank and still. "I don't know what you're intimating."

"I'm not intimating, I'm saying it straight out. You were in the spare room — not the master with the commander. I know you were awake, because your light was on. You heard us relay the information, but despite this close, personal relationship, you didn't come out to express your shock and loss. Why is that, Mrs Skinner?"

"Dallas, I'm sure Mrs Skinner has her reasons." Darcia put a light sting of censure in her voice, then turned a sympathetic smile to Belle. "I'm sorry, Mrs Skinner. The lieutenant is, quite naturally, on edge just now."

"There's no need for you to apologize, Chief Angelo. I understand, and sympathize — to an extent — Lieutenant Dallas's desire to defend and protect her husband."

"Is that what you're doing?" Eve tossed back. "How far would you go? How many close, personal relationships are you willing to sacrifice? Or didn't you have one with Zita Vinter?"

"Zita?" Belle's shoulders jerked, as if from a blow. "What does Zita have to do with any of this?"

"You knew her?"

"She's our godchild, of course I . . . Knew?" Every ounce of color drained out of the lovely face so that the expertly applied enhancements stood out like paint on a doll. "What's happened?"

"She's dead," Eve said flatly. "Murdered early this morning, a few hours after Weeks."

"Dead? *Dead?*" Belle got shakily to her feet, upending her teacup as she floundered for balance. "I can't — I can't talk to you now."

"Want to go after her?" Darcia asked when Belle rushed from the terrace.

"No. Let's give her time to stew. She's scared now. Over what she knows and what she doesn't know." She looked back at Darcia. "We had a pretty good rhythm going there."

"I thought so. But I imagine playing the insensitive, argumentative cop comes naturally to you."

"Just like breathing. Let's blow this tea party and go get a drink." Eve signaled to Peabody and Mira. "Just us girls."

CHAPTER
EIGHT

In the bar, in a wide, plush booth, Eve brooded over a fizzy water. She'd have preferred the good, hard kick of a Zombie, but she wanted a clear head more than the jolt.

"You've got a smooth, sympathetic style," she said to Darcia. "I think she'll talk to you if you stay in that channel."

"So do I."

"Dr Mira here, she's got the same deal. You'd be able to double-team her." Eve glanced toward Mira, who was sipping white wine.

"She was shocked and shaken," Mira began. "First, she'll verify the information about the death of her godchild. When she does, grief will tangle with the shock."

"So, she'll be even more vulnerable to the right questions presented in the right style."

"You're a cold one, Dallas," Darcia said. "I like that about you. I'd be very agreeable to interviewing Belle Skinner with Dr Mira, if that suits the doctor."

"I'm happy to help. I imagine you intend to talk to Skinner again, Eve."

"With the chief's permission."

"Don't start being polite now," Darcia told her. "You'll ruin your image. He won't want to talk to you," she went on. "Whatever his feelings toward you were before, my impression is — after his keynote — he's wrapped you and Roarke together. He hates you both."

"He brought us up at his keynote?"

"Not by name, but by intimation. His inspiring, rather cheerleader-type speech took a turn at the midway point. He went into a tangent on cops who go bad, who forget their primary duties in favor of personal comforts and gains. Gestures, body language . . ." Darcia shrugged. "It was clear he was talking about this place — luxury palaces built on blood and greed, I believe he said — and you. Bedfellows of the wicked. He got very worked up about it, almost evangelical. While there were some who appeared enthusiastic and supportive of that particular line of thought, it seemed to me the bulk of the attendees were uncomfortable — embarrassed or angry."

"He wants to use his keynote to take slaps at me and Roarke, it doesn't worry me." But Eve noticed Peabody staring down into her glass. "Peabody?"

"I think he's sick." She spoke quietly, finally lifted her gaze. "Physically, mentally. I don't think he's real stable. It was hard to watch it happen this morning. He started out sort of, well, eloquent, then it just deteriorated into this rant. I've admired him all my life. It was hard to watch," she repeated. "A lot of the cops who were there stiffened up. You could almost feel layers of respect peeling away. He talked about the murder some, how a young, promising man had become a victim of petty and soulless revenge. How a killer could hide behind a badge instead of being brought to justice by one."

"Pretty pointed," Eve decided.

"A lot of the terrestrial cops walked out then."

"So he's probably a little shaky now himself. I'll take him," Eve said. "Peabody, you track down Feeney, see what other details you can dig out on the two victims and anyone else on-site who's connected with the bust in Atlanta. That fly with you, Chief Angelo?"

Darcia polished off her wine. "It does."

Eve detoured back to the suite first. She wanted a few more details before questioning Skinner again. She never doubted Roarke had already found them.

He was on the 'link when she got there, talking to his head of hotel security. Restless, Eve wandered out onto the terrace and let her mind shuffle the facts, the evidence, the lines of possibilities.

Two dead. Both victims' fathers martyred cops. And those connected to Roarke's father and to Skinner. Murdered in a world of Roarke's making, on a site filled with police officials. It was so neat, it was almost poetic.

A setup from the beginning? It wasn't a crime of impulse but something craftily, coldly planned. Weeks and Vinter had both been sacrifices, pawns placed and disgarded for the greater game. A chess game, all right, she decided. Black king against white, and her gut told her Skinner wouldn't be satisfied with a checkmate.

He wanted blood.

She turned as Roarke stepped out. "In the end, destroying you won't be enough. He's setting you up, step by step, for execution. A lot of weapons on this site. He keeps the pressure on, piles up the circumstantial so there's enough appearance that you might have ordered these hits. All he needs is one soldier willing to take the fall. I'm betting Hayes for that one. Skinner doesn't have much time to pull it off."

"No, he doesn't," Roarke agreed. "I got into his medical records. A year ago he was diagnosed with a rare disorder. It's complicated, but the best I can interpret, it sort of nibbles away at the brain."

"Treatment?"

"Yes, there are some procedures. He's had two — quietly, at a private facility in Zurich. It slowed the process, but in his case . . . He's had complications. A strain on the heart and lungs. Another attempt at correction would kill him. He was given a year. He has, perhaps, three months of that left. And of that three months, two at the outside where he'll continue to be mobile and lucid. He's made arrangements for self-termination."

"That's rough." Eve slipped her hands into her pockets. There was more — she could see it in Roarke's eyes. Something about the way he watched her now. "It plays into the rest. This one event's been stuck in his gut for decades. He wants to clear his books before he checks out. Whatever's eating at his brain has probably made him more unstable, more fanatic and less worried about the niceties. He needs to see you go down before he does. What else? What is it?"

"I went down several more layers in his case file on the bust. His follow-ups, his notes. He believed he'd tracked my father before he'd slipped out of the country again. Skinner used some connections. It was believed that my father headed west and spent a few days among some nefarious associates. In Texas. In Dallas, Eve."

Her stomach clenched, and her heart tripped for several beats. "It's a big place. It doesn't mean . . ."

"The timing's right." He walked to her, ran his hands up and down her arms as if to warm them. "Your father and mine, petty criminals searching for the big score. You were found in that Dallas alley only a few days after Skinner lost my father's trail again."

"You're saying they knew each other, your father and mine."

"I'm saying the circle's too tidy to ignore. I nearly didn't tell you," he added, resting his forehead on hers.

"Give me a minute." She stepped away from him, leaned out on the rail, stared out over the resort. But she was seeing that cold, dirty room, and herself huddled in the corner like an animal. Blood on her hands.

"He had a deal going," she said quietly. "Some deal or other, I think. He wasn't drinking as much — and it was worse for me when he wasn't good and drunk when he came back. And he had some money. Well." She took a deep breath. "Well. It plays out. Do you know what I think?"

"Tell me."

"I think sometimes fate cuts you a break. Like it says, okay, you've had enough of that crap, so it's time you fell into something nice. See what you make out of it." She turned back to him then. "We're making something out of it. Whatever they were to us, or to each other, it's what we are now that counts."

"Darling Eve. I adore you."

"Then you'll do me a favor. Keep yourself scarce for the next couple of hours. I don't want to give Skinner any opportunities. I need to talk to him, and he won't talk if you're with me."

"Agreed, with one condition. You go wired." He took a small jeweled pin from his pocket, attached it to her lapel. "I'll monitor from here."

"It's illegal to record without all parties' knowledge and permission unless you have proper authorization."

"Is it really?" He kissed her. "That's what you get for bedding down with bad companions."

"Heard about that, did you?"

"Just as I heard that a large portion of your fellow cops walked out of the speech. Your reputation stands, Lieutenant. I imagine your seminar tomorrow will be packed."

"My . . . Shit! I forgot. I'm not thinking about it," she muttered on the way out. "Not thinking about it."

She slipped into the conference room where Skinner was leading a seminar on tactics. It was some relief to realize she'd missed the lecture and had come in during the question-and-answer period. There were a lot of long looks in her direction as she walked down the side of the room and found a seat halfway from the back.

She scoped out the setup. Skinner on stage at the podium, Hayes standing to his back and his right, at attention. Two other personal security types on his other side.

Excessive, she thought, and obviously so. The message was that the location, the situation, posed personal jeopardy for Skinner; but he was taking precautions and doing his job.

Very neat.

She raised her hand, and was ignored. Five questions passed until she simply got to her feet and addressed him. And as she rose, she noted Hayes slide a hand inside his jacket.

She knew every cop in the room caught the gesture. The room went dead quiet.

"Commander Skinner, a position of command regularly requires you to send men into situations where loss of life, civilian and departmental, is a primary risk. In such cases, do you find it more beneficial to the operation to set personal feelings for your men aside, or to use those feelings to select the team?"

"Every man who picks up a badge does so acknowledging he will give his life if need be to serve and protect. Every commander must respect that acknowledgment. Personal feelings must be weighed, in order to select the right man for the right situation. This is a matter of experience and the accumulation, through years and that experience, of recognizing the best dynamic for each given op. But personal feelings

— i.e., emotional attachments, private connections, friendships, or animosities — must never color the decision."

"So, as commander, you'd have no problem sacrificing a close personal friend or connection to the success of the op?"

His color came up. And the tremor she had noticed in his hand became more pronounced. " 'Sacrificing', Lieutenant Dallas? A poor choice of words. Cops aren't lambs being sent to slaughter. Not passive sacrifices to the greater good, but active, dedicated soldiers in the fight for justice."

"Soldiers are sacrificed in battle. Acceptable losses."

"No loss is acceptable." His bunched fist pounded the podium. "Necessary, but not acceptable. Every man who has fallen under my command weighs on me. Every child left without a father is my responsibility. Command requires this, and that the commander be strong enough to bear the burden."

"And does command, in your opinion, require restitution for those losses?"

"It does, Lieutenant. There is no justice without payment."

"For the children of the fallen? And for the children of those who escaped the hand of justice? In your opinion."

"Blood speaks to blood." His voice began to rise, and to tremble. "If you were more concerned with justice than with your own personal choices, you wouldn't need to ask the question."

"Justice is my concern, Commander. It appears we have different definitions of the term. Do you think your god-daughter was the best choice for this operation? Does her death weigh on you now, or does it balance the other losses?"

"You're not fit to speak her name. You've whored your badge. You're a disgrace. Don't think your husband's money or threats will stop me from using all my influence to have that badge taken from you."

"I don't stand behind Roarke any more than he stands behind me." She kept talking as Hayes stepped forward and laid a hand on Skinner's shoulder. "I don't stand on yesterday's business. Two people are dead here and now. That's my priority, Commander. Justice for them is my concern."

Hayes stepped in front of Skinner. "The seminar is over. Commander Skinner thanks you for attending and regrets Lieutenant Dallas's disruption of the question-and-answer period."

People shuffled, rose. Eve saw Skinner leaving, flanked by the two guards.

"Ask me," someone commented near her, "these seminars could use more fucking disruptions."

She made her way toward the front and came up toe to toe with Hayes.

"I've got two more questions for the commander."

"I said the seminar's over. And so's your little show."

She felt the crowd milling around them, some edging close enough to hear. "You see, that's funny. I thought I came in on the show. Does he run it, Hayes, or do you?"

"Commander Skinner is a great man. Great men often need protection from whores."

A cop moved in, poked Hayes on the shoulder. "You're gonna want to watch the name-calling, man."

"Thanks." Eve acknowledged him with a nod. "I've got it."

"Don't like play cops calling a badge a whore." He stepped back, but he hovered.

"While you're protecting the great man," Eve continued, "you might want to remember that two of his front-line soldiers are in the morgue."

"Is that a threat, Lieutenant?"

"Hell, no. It's a fact, Hayes. Just like it's a fact that both of them had fathers who died under Skinner's command. What about your father?"

Furious color slashed across his cheekbones. "You know nothing of my father, and you have no right to speak of him."

"Just giving you something to think about. For some reason I get the feeling that I'm more interested in finding out who put those bodies in the morgue than you or your great man. And because I am, I will find out — before this show breaks down and moves on. That one's a promise."

CHAPTER
NINE

If she couldn't get to Skinner, Eve thought, she'd get to
Skinner's wife. And if Angelo and Mira hadn't softened
and soothed enough, that was too fucking bad.
Damned if she was going to tiptoe around weepy
women and dying men, then have to turn the case over
to the interplanetary boys.

It was her case, and she meant to close it.

She knew that part of her anger and urgency
stemmed from the information Roarke had given her.
His father, hers, Skinner, and a team of dead cops.
Skinner was right about one thing, she thought as she
headed for his suite. Blood spoke to blood.

The blood of the dead had always spoken to her.

Her father and Roarke's had both met a violent end.
That was all the justice she could offer to the badges
lost so many years before. But there were two bodies in
cold boxes. For those, whatever they'd done, she would
stand.

She knocked, waited impatiently. It was Darcia who
opened the door and sent Eve an apologetic little
wince.

"She's a mess," Darcia whispered. "Mira's patting
her hand, letting her cry over her goddaughter. It's a

good foundation, but we haven't been able to build on it yet."

"Any objections to me giving the foundation a shake?"

Darcia studied her, pursed her lips. "We can try it that way, but I wouldn't shake too hard. She shatters, we're back to square one with her."

With a nod, Eve stepped in. Mira was on the sofa with Belle, and was indeed holding her hand. A teapot, cups, and countless tissues littered the table in front of them. Belle was weeping softly into a fresh one.

"Mrs Skinner, I'm sorry for your loss." Eve sat in a chair by the sofa, leaned into the intimacy. She kept her voice quiet, sympathetic, and waited until Belle lifted swollen, red-rimmed eyes to hers.

"How can you speak of her? Your husband's responsible."

"My husband and I were nearly blown to bits by an explosive device on Zita Vinter's apartment door. A device set by her killer. Follow the dots."

"Who else had cause to kill Zita?"

"That's what we want to find out. She sabotaged the security cameras the night Weeks was murdered."

"I don't believe that." Belle balled the tissue into her fist. "Zita would never be a party to murder. She was a lovely young woman. Caring and capable."

"And devoted to your husband."

"Why shouldn't she be?" Belle's voice rose as she got to her feet. "He stepped in when her father died. Gave her his time and attention, helped with her education. He'd have done anything for her."

"And she for him?"

Belle's lips quivered, and she sat again, as if her legs quivered as well. "She would never be a party to murder. He would never ask it of her."

"Maybe she didn't know. Maybe she was just asked to deal with the cameras and nothing else. Mrs Skinner, your husband's dying." Eve saw Belle jerk, shudder. "He doesn't have much time left, and the loss of his men is preying on him as he prepares for death. Can you sit there and tell me his behavior over the last several months has been rational?"

"I won't discuss my husband's condition with you."

"Mrs Skinner, do you believe Roarke's responsible for something his father did? Something this man did when Roarke was a child, three thousand miles away?"

She watched tears swim into Belle's eyes again, and leaned in. Pressed. "The man used to beat Roarke half to death for sport. Do you know what it feels like to be hit with fists, or a stick, or whatever the hell's handy — and by the person who's supposed to take care of you? By law, by simple morality. Do you know what it's like to be bloody and bruised and helpless to fight back?"

"No." The tears spilled over. "No."

"Does that child have to pay for the viciousness of the man?"

"The sins of the fathers . . ." Belle began, then stopped. "No." Wearily, she wiped her wet cheeks. "No, Lieutenant, I don't believe that. But I know what it has cost my husband, what happened before, what was lost. I know how it's haunted him — this good, good man, this honorable man who has dedicated his life to his badge and everything it stands for."

"He can't exorcise his ghosts by destroying the son of the man who made them. You know that, too."

"He would never harm Zita, or Reggie. He loved them as if they were his own. But . . ." She turned to Mira again, gripped her hands fiercely. "He's so ill — in body, mind, spirit. I don't know how to help him. I don't know how long I can stand watching him die in stages. I'm prepared to let him go because the pain — sometimes it's so horrible. And he won't let me in. He won't share the bed with me, or his thoughts, his fears. It's as if he's divorcing me, bit by bit. I can't stop it."

"For some, death is a solitary act," Mira said gently. "Intimate and private. It's hard to love someone and stand aside while they take those steps alone."

"He agreed to apply for self-termination for me." Belle sighed. "He doesn't believe in it. He believes a man should stand up to whatever he's handed and see it through. I'm afraid he's not thinking clearly any longer. There are moments . . ."

She steadied her breathing and looked back at Eve. "There are rages, swings of mood. The medication may be partially responsible. He's never shared the job with me to any great extent. But I know that for months now, perhaps longer, Roarke has been a kind of obsession to him. As have you. You chose the devil over duty."

She closed her eyes a moment. "I'm a cop's wife, Lieutenant. I believe in that duty, and I see it all over you. He would see it, too, if he weren't so ill. I swear to you he didn't kill Reggie or Zita. But they may have been killed for him."

"Belle." Mira offered her another tissue. "You want to help your husband, to ease his pain. Tell Lieutenant Dallas and Chief Angelo what you know, what you feel. No one knows your husband's heart and mind the way you do."

"It'll shatter him. If he has to face this, it'll destroy him. Fathers and sons," she said softly, then buried her face in the tissue. "Oh, dear God."

"Hayes." It clicked for Eve like a link on a chain. "Hayes didn't lose a father during the bust. He's Commander Skinner's son."

"A single indiscretion." Tears choked Belle's voice when she lifted her head again. "During a bump in a young marriage. And so much of it my fault. My fault," she repeated, turning her pleading gaze to Mira. "I was impatient, and angry, that so much of his time, his energies went into his work. I'd married a cop, but I hadn't been willing to accept all that that meant — all it meant to a man like Douglas."

"It isn't easy to share a marriage with duty." Mira poured more tea. "Particularly when duty is what defines the partner. You were young."

"Yes." Gratitude spilled into Belle's voice as she lifted her cup. "Young and selfish, and I've done everything in my power to make up for it since. I loved him terribly, and wanted all of him. I couldn't have that, so I pushed and prodded, then I stepped away from him. All or nothing. Well. He's a proud man, and I was stubborn. We separated for six months, and

224

during that time he turned to someone else. I can't blame him for it."

"And she got pregnant," Eve prompted.

"Yes. He never kept it from me. He never lied or tried to hide it from me. He's an honorable man." Her tone turned fierce when she looked at Eve.

"Does Hayes know?"

"Of course. Of course he knows. Douglas would never shirk his responsibilities. He provided financial support. We worked out an arrangement with the woman, and she agreed to raise the child and keep his paternity private. There was no point, no point at all in making the matter public and complicating Douglas's career, shadowing his reputation."

"So you paid for his . . . indiscretion."

"You're a hard woman, aren't you, Lieutenant? No mistakes in your life? No regrets?"

"Plenty of them. But a child — a man — might have some problem being considered a mistake. A regret."

"Douglas has been nothing but kind and generous and responsible with Bryson. He's given him everything."

Everything except his name, Eve thought. How much would that matter? "Did he give him orders to kill, Mrs Skinner? Orders to frame Roarke for murder?"

"Absolutely not. Absolutely not. But Bryson is . . . perhaps he's overly devoted to Douglas. In the past several months, Douglas has turned to him too often, and perhaps, when Bryson was growing up, Douglas set standards that were too high, too harsh for a young boy."

225

"Hayes would need to prove himself to his father."

"Yes. Bryson's hard, Lieutenant. Hard and cold-blooded. You'd understand that, I think. Douglas — he's ill. And his moods, his obsession with what happened all those years ago is eating at him as viciously as his illness does. I've heard him rage, as if there's something else inside him. And during the rage he said something had to be done, some payment made, whatever the cost. That there were times the law had to make room for blood justice. Death for death. I heard him talking with Bryson, months ago, about this place. That Roarke had built it on the bones of martyred cops. That he would never rest until it, and Roarke, were destroyed. That if he died before he could avenge those who were lost, his legacy to his son was that duty."

"Pick him up." Eve swung to Darcia. "Have your people pick Hayes up."

"Already on it," Darcia answered as she switched on her communicator.

"He doesn't know." Belle got slowly to her feet. "Or he's not allowing himself to know. Douglas is convinced that Roarke's responsible for what's happened here. Convinced himself that you're part of it, Lieutenant. His mind isn't what it was. He's dying by inches. This will finish him. Have pity."

She thought of the dead, and thought of the dying. "Ask yourself what he would have done, Mrs Skinner, if he were standing in my place now. Dr Mira will stay with you."

She headed out with Darcia, waited until they were well down the hall. "There should be a way to separate him from Skinner before we bag him. Take him quietly."

Darcia called for the elevator. "You're some ruthless hardass, aren't you, Dallas?"

"If Skinner didn't give him a direct order, there's no point in smearing him with Hayes, or making the arrest while he's around. Christ, he's a dead man already," she snapped when Darcia said nothing. "What's the fucking point of dragging him into it and destroying half a century of service?"

"None."

"I can request another interview with Skinner, draw him away far enough for you to make the collar."

"You're giving up the collar?" Darcia asked in a shocked voice as they stepped onto the elevator.

"It was never mine."

"The hell it wasn't. But I'll take it," Darcia added cheerfully. "How'd you click to the relationship between Skinner and Hayes?"

"Fathers. The case is lousy with them. You got one?"

"A father? Doesn't everyone?"

"Depends on your point of view." She stepped off the car on the main lobby level. "I'm going to round up Peabody, give you a chance to coordinate your team." She checked her wrist unit. "Fifteen minutes ought to . . . Well, well. Look who's holding court in the lobby lounge."

Darcia tracked, studied the group crowded at two tables. "Skinner looks to have recovered his composure."

"The man likes an audience. It probably pumps him up more than his meds. We could play it this way. We go over, and I apologize for disrupting the seminar. Distract Skinner, get him talking. You tell Hayes you'd like to have a word with him about Weeks. Don't want to disturb Skinner with routine questions and blah, blah. Can you take him on your own?"

Darcia gave her a bland stare. "Could you?"

"Okay, then. Let's do it. Quick and quiet."

They were halfway across the lobby when Hayes spotted them. Two beats later, he was running.

"Goddamn it, goddamn it. He's got cop instincts. Circle that way," Eve ordered, then charged the crowd. She vaulted the smooth gold rail that separated the lounge from the lobby. People shouted, spilled back. Glassware crashed as a table overturned. She caught a glimpse of Hayes as he swung through a door behind the bar.

She leaped the bar, ignoring the curses of the servers and patrons. Bottles smashed, and there was a sudden, heady scent of top-grade liquor. Her weapon was in her hand when she hit the door with her shoulder.

The bar kitchen was full of noise. A cook droid was sprawled on the floor in the narrow aisle, its head jerking from the damage done by the fall. She stumbled over it, and the blast from Hayes's laser sang over her head.

Rather than right herself, she rolled and came up behind a stainless-steel cabinet.

"Give it up, Hayes. Where are you going to go? There are innocent people in here. Drop your weapon."

228

"Nobody's innocent." He fired again, and the line of heat scored across the floor and finished off the droid.

"This isn't what your father wants. He doesn't want more dead piling up at his feet."

"There's no price too high for duty." A shelf of dinnerware exploded beside her, showering her with shards.

"Screw this." She sent a line of fire over her head, rolled to the left. She came up weapon first and cursed again as she lost the target around a corner.

Someone was screaming. Someone else was crying. Keeping low, she set off in pursuit. She turned toward the sound of another blast and saw a fire erupt in a pile of linens.

"Somebody take care of that!" she shouted and turned the next corner. Saw the exit door. "Shit!"

He'd blasted the locks, effectively sealing it. In frustration she rammed it, gave it a couple of solid kicks, and didn't budge it an inch.

Holstering her weapon, she made her way back out the mess and smoke. Without much hope, she ran through the lobby, out the main doors to scan the streets. By the time she'd made it to the corner, Darcia was heading back.

"Lost him. Son of a bitch. He had a block and a half on me." Darcia jammed her own weapon home. "I'd never have caught him on foot in these damn shoes. I've got an APB out. We'll net the bastard."

"Fucker smelled the collar." Furious with herself, Eve spun in a circle. "I didn't give him enough credit. He knocked some people around in the bar kitchen.

Offed a droid, started a fire. He's fast and smart and slick. And he's goddamn mean on top of it."

"We'll net him," Darcia repeated.

"Damn right we will."

CHAPTER
TEN

"Lieutenant."

Eve winced, turned and watched Roarke walk toward her. "Guess you heard we had a little incident."

"I believe I'll just see to some damage control." Humor cut through the anger on Darcia's face. "Excuse me."

"Are you hurt?" Roarke asked Eve.

"No. But you've got a dead droid in the bar kitchen. I didn't kill it, in case you're wondering. There was a little fire, too. But I didn't start it. The ceiling damage, that's on me. And some of the, you know, breakage and stuff."

"I see." He studied the elegant facade of the hotel. "I'm sure the guests and the staff found it all very exciting. The ones who don't sue me should enjoy telling the story to their friends and relations for quite some time. Since I'll be contacting my attorneys to alert them to a number of civil suits heading our way, perhaps you'd take a moment to fill me in on why I have a dead droid, a number of hysterical guests, screaming staff, and a little fire in the bar kitchen."

"Sure. Why don't we round up Peabody and Feeney, then I can just run through it once?"

"No, I think I'd like to know now. Let's just have a bit of a walk." He took her arm.

"I don't have time to —"

"Make it."

He led her around the hotel, through the side gardens, the patio cafe, wound through one of the pool areas and into a private elevator while he listened to her report.

"So your intentions were to spare Skinner's feelings and reputation."

"Didn't work out, but, yeah, to a point. Hayes made us first glance." The minute she was in the suite, she popped open a bottle of water, glugged. Until that moment she hadn't realized the smoke had turned her throat into a raw desert of thirst. "Should've figured it. Now he's in the wind, and that's on me, too."

"He won't get off the station."

"No, he won't get off. But he might take it in mind to do some damage while he's loose. I'll need to look at the maps and plans for the resort. We'll do a computer analysis, ear-mark the spots he'd be most likely to go to ground."

"I'll take care of that. I can do it faster," he said before she could object. "You need a shower. You smell of smoke."

She lifted her arm, sniffed it. "Yeah, I guess I do. Since you're being so helpful, tag Peabody and Feeney, will you? I want this manhunt coordinated."

"Too many places for him to hide." An hour later, Eve scowled at the wall screens and the locations the computer had selected. "I'm wondering, too, if he had some sort of backup transpo in case this turned on him, someone he's bribed to smuggle him off-site. If he gets off this station, he could go any fucking where."

"I can work with Angelo on running that angle down," Feeney said. "And some e-maneuvering can bog down anything scheduled to leave the site for a good twenty-four hours."

"Good thinking. Keep in touch, okay?"

"Will do." He headed out, rattling a bag of almonds.

"Roarke knows the site best. He'll take me around to the specified locations. We'll split them up with Angelo's team."

"Do I coordinate from here?" Peabody asked.

"Not exactly. I need you to work with Mira. Make sure Skinner and his wife stay put and report if Hayes contacts them. Then there's this other thing."

"Yes, sir." Peabody looked up from her memo book.

"If we don't bag him tonight, you'll have to cover for me in the morning."

"Cover for you?"

"I've got the notes and whatever in here." Eve tossed her PPC into Peabody's lap.

"Notes?" Peabody stared at the little unit in horror. "Your seminar? Oh, no, sir. Uh-uh. Dallas, I'm not giving your seminar."

"Just think of yourself as backup," Eve suggested. "Roarke?" She walked to the door and through it, leaving Peabody sputtering.

"Just how much don't you want to give that seminar tomorrow?" Roarke wondered.

"I don't have to answer that until I've been given the revised Miranda warning." Eve rolled her shoulders and would have sworn she felt weight spilling off them. "Sometimes things just work out perfect, don't they?"

"Ask Peabody that in the morning."

With a laugh, she stepped into the elevator. "Let's go hunting."

They hit every location, even overlapping into Angelo's portion. It was a long, tedious, and exacting process. Later she would think that the operation had given her a more complete view of the scope of Roarke's pet project. The hotels, casinos, theaters, restaurants, the shops and businesses. The houses and buildings, the beaches and parks. The sheer sweep of the world he'd created was more than she'd imagined.

While impressive, it made the job at hand next to impossible.

It was after three in the morning when she gave it up for the night and stumbled to bed. "We'll find him tomorrow. His face is on every screen on-site. The minute he tries to buy any supplies, we'll tag him. He has to sleep, he has to eat."

"So do you." In bed, Roarke drew her against him. "Turn it off, Lieutenant. Tomorrow's soon enough."

"He won't go far." Her voice thickened with sleep. "He needs to finish it and get his father's praises. Legacies. Bloody legacies. I spent my life running from mine."

"I know." Roarke brushed the top of her head with his lips as she fell into sleep. "So have I."

This time it was he who dreamed, as he rarely did, of the alleyways of Dublin. Of himself, a young boy, too thin, with sharp eyes, nimble fingers, and fast feet. A belly too often empty.

The smell of garbage gone over, and whiskey gone stale, and the cold of the rain that gleefully seeped into bone.

He saw himself in one of those alleyways, staring down at his father, who lay with that garbage gone over, and smelled of that whiskey gone stale. And smelled, too, of death — the blood and the shit that spewed out of a man at his last moments. The knife had still been in his throat, and his eyes — filmed-over blue — were open and staring back at the boy he'd made.

He remembered, quite clearly, speaking.

Well now, you bastard, someone's done for ya. And here I thought it would be me one day who had the pleasure of that.

Without a qualm, he'd crouched and searched through the pockets for any coin or items that might be pawned or traded. There'd been nothing, but then again, there never had been much. He'd considered, briefly, taking the knife. But he'd liked the idea of it where it was too much to bother.

He'd stood then, at the age of twelve, with bruises still fresh and aching from the last beating those dead hands had given him.

And he'd spat. And he'd run.

He was up before she was, as usual. Eve studied him as she grabbed her first cup of coffee. It was barely seven A.M. "You look tired."

He continued to study the stock reports on one screen and the computer analysis of potential locations on another. "Do I? I suppose I could've slept better."

When she crouched in front of him, laid a hand on his thigh, he looked at her. And sighed. She could read him well enough, he thought, his cop.

Just as he could read her, and her worry for him.

"I wonder," he began, "and I don't care to, who did me the favor of sticking that knife in him. Someone, I think, who was part of the cartel. He'd have been paid, you see, and there was nothing in his pockets. Not a fucking punt or pence on him, nor in the garbage hole we lived in. So they'd have taken it, whatever he hadn't already whored or drank or simply pissed away."

"Does it matter who?"

"Not so very much, no. But it makes me wonder." He nearly didn't say the rest, but simply having her listen soothed him. "He had my face. I forget that most times, remember that I've made myself, myself. But Christ, I have the look of him."

She slid into his lap, brushed her hands through his hair. "I don't think so." And kissed him.

"We've made each other in the end, haven't we, Darling Eve? Two lost souls into one steady unit."

"Guess we have. It's good."

He stroked his cheek against hers, and felt the fatigue wash away. "Very good."

She held on another minute, then drew back. "That's enough sloppy stuff. I've got work to do."

"When it's done, why don't we get really sloppy, you and I?"

"I can get behind that." She rose to contact Darcia and get an update on the manhunt.

"Not a sign of him anywhere," Eve told Roarke, then began to pace. "Feeney took care of transpo. Nothing's left the station. We've got him boxed in, but it's a big box with lots of angles. I need Skinner. Nobody's going to know him as well as Skinner."

"Hayes is his son," Roarke reminded her. "Do you think he'd help you?"

"Depends on how much cop is left in him. Come with me," she said. "He needs to see us both. He needs to deal with it."

He looked haggard, Eve thought. His skin was gray and pasty. How much was grief, how much illness, she didn't know. The combination of the two, she imagined, would finish him.

But, she noted, he'd put on a suit, and he wore his precinct pin in the lapel.

He brushed aside, with some impatience, his wife's attempt to block Eve.

"Stop fussing, Belle. Lieutenant." His gaze skimmed over Roarke, but he couldn't make himself address the man. "I want you to know I've contacted my attorneys on Hayes's behalf. I believe you and Chief Angelo have made a serious error in judgment."

"No, you don't, Commander. You've been a cop too long. I appreciate the difficulty of your position, but Hayes is the prime suspect in two murders, in sabotage, in a conspiracy to implicate Roarke in those murders. He injured bystanders while fleeing and caused considerable property damage. He also fired his weapon at a police officer. He's currently evading arrest."

"There's an explanation."

"Yes, I believe there is. He's picked up his father's banner, Commander, and he's carrying it where I don't think you intended it to go. You told me yesterday no losses are acceptable. Did you mean it?"

"The pursuit of justice often . . . In the course of duty, we . . ." He looked helplessly at his wife. "Belle, I never meant — Reggie, Zita. Have I killed them?"

"No, no." She went to him quickly, wrapped her arms around him. And he seemed to shrink into her. "It's not your fault. It's not your doing."

"If you want justice for them, Commander, help me. Where would he go? What would he do next?"

"I don't know. Do you think I haven't agonized over it through the night?"

"He hasn't slept," Belle told her. "He won't take his pain medication. He needs to rest."

"I confided in him," Skinner continued. "I shared my thoughts, my beliefs, my anger. I wanted him to carry on my mission. Not this way." Skinner sank into a chair. "Not this way, but I beat the path. I can't deny that. Your father killed for sport, for money, for the hell of it," he said to Roarke. "He didn't even know the names of the people he murdered. I look at you and see him. You grew out of him."

"I did." Roarke nodded. "And everything I've done since has been in spite of him. You can't hate him as much as I can, Commander. No matter how hard you try, you'll never reach my measure of it. But I can't live on that hate. And I'm damned if I'll die on it. Will you?"

"I've used it to keep me alive these past months." Skinner looked down at his hands. "It's ruined me. My son is a thorough man. He'll have a back door. Someone inside who'll help him gain access to the hotel. He'll need it to finish what he started."

"Assassinate Roarke?"

"No, Lieutenant. Payment would be dearer than that. It's you he'll aim for." He lifted a hand to a face that had gone clammy. "To take away what his target cherishes most."

When he hissed in pain, Eve stepped forward. "You need medical attention, Commander. You need to be in the hospital."

"No hospitals. No health centers. Try to take him alive, Dallas. I want him to get the help he needs."

"You have to go." Belle stepped in. "He can't take any more of this."

"I'll send Dr Mira." Even as Eve spoke, Skinner slumped in the chair.

"He's unconscious." Roarke instinctively loosened Skinner's tie. "His breathing's very shallow."

"Don't touch him! Let me —" Belle jerked back as her eyes met Roarke's. She took a long, deep breath. "I'm sorry. Could you help me, please? Take him into his bedroom. If you'd call for Dr Mira, Lieutenant Dallas, I'd be grateful."

"His body's wearing down," Eve said once Skinner was settled in the bedroom with Mira in attendance.

"Maybe it's better all around if he goes before we take Hayes."

"His body was already worn down," Roarke corrected. "But he's let go of his reason to live."

"There's nothing to do but leave him to Mira. The computer didn't think Hayes would come back to the hotel. Skinner does. I'm going with Skinner. Hayes wants me, and he knows Skinner's on borrowed time so he has to move fast." She checked her wrist unit. "Looks like I'm going to give that damn seminar after all."

"And make yourself a target?"

"With plenty of shield. We'll coordinate your security people and Angelo's and pluck him like a goose if he tries for a hit here." She started out, pulling a borrowed communicator out of her pocket.

Then drew her weapon as she saw Hayes step out of the stairway door at the end of the corridor.

"Stop!" She pounded after him when he ducked back into the stairwell. "Get to security!" Eve shouted at Roarke. "Track him!"

Roarke shoved through the door ahead of her. The weapon in his hand was illegal. "No. You track him."

Since cursing was a waste of time, she raced down the stairs with him. "Subject sighted," she called through the communicator as they streaked down the stairs. "Heading down southeast stairwell, now between floors twenty-one and twenty. Moving fast. Consider subject armed and dangerous."

She clicked the communicator off before she spoke to Roarke. "Don't kill him. Don't fire that thing unless there's no choice."

A blast hit the landing seconds before their feet. "Such as now?" Roarke commented.

But it was Eve who fired, leaning over the railing and turning the steps below into rubble. Caught in midstride, Hayes tried to swing back, bolt for the door, but his momentum skewed his balance.

He went down hard on the smoking, broken steps.

And Angelo shoved through the door, weapon gripped in both hands.

"Trying to take my collar, Dallas?"

"All yours." Eve stepped down, onto the weapon that had flown out of Hayes's hand. "Two people dead. For what?" she asked Hayes. "Was it worth it?"

His mouth and his leg were bleeding. He swiped at the blood on his chin while his eyes burned into hers. "No. I should've been more direct. I should've just blown you to hell right away and watched the bastard you fuck bleed over you. That would've been worth everything, knowing he'd live with the kind of pain his father caused. The commander could've died at peace knowing I'd found his justice. I wanted to give him more."

"Did you give Weeks or Vinter a choice?" Eve demanded. "Did you tell them they were going to die for the cause?"

"Command isn't required to explain. They honored their fathers, as I honor mine. There's no other choice."

"You signaled Weeks to move in on me, and he didn't have a clue what it was going to cost him. You had Vinter sabotage the cameras, and when she realized why, you killed her."

"They were necessary losses. Justice requires payment. You were going to be my last gift to him. You in a cage," he said to Roarke. "You in a coffin." He smiled at Eve when he said it. "Why aren't you giving your seminar, Lieutenant? Why the hell aren't you where you're scheduled to be?"

"I had a conflict of . . ." She shot to her feet. "Oh, God. Peabody."

She charged through the door and out into the corridor. "What floor? What floor?"

"This way." Roarke grabbed her hand, pulled her toward the elevator. "Down to four," he said. "We'll head left. Second door on the right takes us behind the stage area."

"Explosives. He likes explosives." She dragged out her communicator again as she willed the elevator to hurry. "She's turned hers off. Son of a bitch! Any officer, any officer, clear Conference Room D immediately. Clear the area of all personnel. Possible explosive device. Alert Explosive Division. Clear that area now!"

She was through the door and streaking to the left.

I sent her there, was all she could think. And I smirked about it.

Oh, God, please.

There was a roaring in her ears that was either her own rush of blood, the noise of the audience, or the shouted orders to clear.

But she spotted Peabody standing behind the podium and leaped the three steps on the side of the stage. Leaped again the minute her feet hit the ground and, hitting her aide mid-body, shot them both into the air and into a bruised and tangled heap on the floor.

She sucked in her breath, then lost it again as Roarke landed on top of her.

The explosion rang in her ears, sent the floor under her shaking. She felt the mean heat of it spew over her like a wave that sent the three of them rolling in one ball toward the far edge of the stage.

Debris rained over them, some of it flaming. Dimly she heard running feet, shouts, and the sizzling hiss of a fire.

For the second time in two days, she was drenched with the spray of overhead sprinklers.

"Are you all right?" Roarke said in her ear.

"Yeah, yeah. Peabody." Coughing, eyes stinging with smoke, Eve eased back, saw her aide's pale face, glassy eyes. "You okay?"

"Think so." She blinked. "'Cept you've got two heads, Dallas, and one of them's Roarke's. It's the prettiest. And I think you've really gained some weight." She smiled vaguely and passed out.

"Got herself a nice concussion," Eve decided, then turned her head so her nose bumped Roarke's. "You are pretty, though. Now get the hell off me. This is seriously undignified."

"Absolutely, Lieutenant."

While the med-techs tended to Peabody, and the Explosives Division cordoned off the scene, Eve sat outside the conference room and drank the coffee some unnamed and beloved soul had handed her.

She was soaked to the skin, filthy, had a few cuts, a medley of bruises. She figured her ears might stop ringing by Christmas.

But all in all, she felt just fine.

"You're going to have a few repairs on this dump of yours," she told Roarke.

"Just can't take you anywhere, can I?"

She smiled, then got to her feet as Darcia approached. "Hayes is in custody. He's waived his right to attorney. My opinion, he'll end up in a facility for violent offenders, mental defectives. He's not going to serve time in a standard cage. He's warped. If it's any consolation, he was very disappointed to hear you aren't splattered all over what's left of that stage in there."

"Can't always get what you want."

"Hell of a way to skate out of giving a workshop, though. Have to hand it to you."

"Whatever works."

Sobering, Darcia turned. "We beat interplanetary deadline. Thanks."

"I won't say 'any time'."

"I'll have a full report for your files by the end of the day," she said to Roarke. "I hope your next visit is less . . . complicated," she added.

"It was an experience watching you in action, Chief Angelo. I'm confident Olympus is in good hands."

"Count on it. You know, Dallas, you look like you could use a nice resort vacation." She shot out that brilliant smile. "See you around."

"She's got a smart mouth. I've got to admire that. I'm going to check on Peabody," she began, then stopped when she saw Mira coming toward her.

"He's gone," Mira said simply. "He had time to say good-bye to his wife, and to ask me to tell you that he was wrong. Blood doesn't always tell. I witnessed the termination. He left life with courage and dignity. He asked me if you would stand in the way of his departmental service and burial."

"What did you tell him?"

"I told him that blood doesn't always tell. Character does. I'm going back to his wife now."

"Tell her I'm sorry for her loss, and that law enforcement has lost one of its great heroes today."

Mira leaned over to kiss Eve's cheek, smiling when Eve squirmed. "You have a good heart."

"And clear vision," Roarke added when Mira walked away.

"Clear vision?"

"To see through the dreck and the shadows to the core of the man."

"Nobody gets through life without fucking up. He gave fifty years to the badge. It wasn't all what it should've been, but it was fifty years. Anyway." She shook off sentiment. "I've got to check on Peabody."

Roarke took her hand, kissed it. "We'll go check on Peabody. Then we'll talk about that nice resort vacation."

In a pig's eye, she thought. She was going home as soon as humanly possible. The streets of New York were resort enough for her.

Other titles published by Ulverscroft:

OBSESSION IN DEATH

J. D. Robb

Eve Dallas is used to unwanted attention. Famous for her high-profile cases and her marriage to billionaire businessman Roarke, she has learned to deal with intense public scrutiny and media gossip. But now Eve has become the object of a singular and deadly obsession. She has an "admirer", who just can't stop thinking about her. Who is convinced they have a special bond. Who is planning to kill for her — again and again . . . With time against her, Eve is forced to participate in a delicate — and dangerous — psychological dance. Because the killer is desperate for something Eve can never provide: approval. And once that becomes clear, Eve knows her own life will be at risk, along with those she cares about the most.

CHAOS IN DEATH AND POSSESSION IN DEATH

J. D. Robb

In *Chaos in Death*, when eye-witness testimony paints the killer as a green-skinned monster with swollen red eyes and goblin ears, even Eve Dallas is shaken. But as she gets closer, the trail suggests something far more disturbing — someone is playing with science . . . While in *Possession in Death*, after a Gypsy woman whispers her dying words to Eve Dallas, strange things begin to happen. Unable to concentrate on anything, Eve realises that in order to reclaim her mind, she must find the woman's great-granddaughter — one of a string of young missing girls forgotten, or ignored, by all.

HAUNTED IN DEATH AND ETERNITY IN DEATH

J. D. Robb

Lieutenant Eve Dallas doesn't believe in ghosts. But in *Haunted in Death*, when a very recent corpse shows up in an abandoned nightclub, alongside the bones of famous missing singer Bobbie Bray, everyone is spooked. Did Bobbie's ghost finally get her revenge, or is there a more earthly explanation? While in *Eternity in Death*, when notorious It-girl Tiara Kent is found dead in her plush Manhattan apartment, the murder looks to everyone like a vampire attack — everyone but the practical Lieutenant Eve Dallas. Discovering Tiara's secret lover, Eve and her team are led on a chase into the darkest corners of the city and deep into their own fears.

FESTIVE IN DEATH

J. D. Robb

It's Christmas, but Lieutenant Eve Dallas is in no mood to celebrate. While her charismatic husband Roarke plans a huge, glittering party, Eve has murder on her mind. The victim — personal trainer Trey Ziegler — was trouble in life and is causing even more problems in death. Vain, unfaithful and vindictive, Trey had cultivated a lot of enemies. Which means Eve has a lot of potential suspects. And when she and Detective Peabody uncover Trey's sinister secret, the case takes a deadly turn. Christmas may be a festival of light, but Eve and Roarke will be forced once more down a very dark path in their hunt for the truth.

CONCEALED IN DEATH

J. D. Robb

There is nothing unusual about billionaire Roarke supervising work on his new property — but when he takes a ceremonial swing at the first wall to be knocked down, he uncovers the body of a girl. And then another — in fact, twelve dead girls concealed behind a false wall.

Luckily for Roarke, he is married to the best police lieutenant in town. Eve Dallas is determined to find the killer — especially when she discovers that the building used to be a sanctuary for delinquent teenagers and the parallel with her past as a young runaway hits hard.

As the girls' identities are slowly unravelled by the department's crack forensic team, Eve and her staunch sidekick Peabody get closer to the shocking truth.

RITUAL IN DEATH AND MISSING IN DEATH

J. D. Robb

A duo of two superb short stories featuring celebrated lieutenant, Eve Dallas

Ritual in Death: When a naked, knife-wielding man who thinks he has killed someone crashes a glamorous ball she's attending, Lieutenant Eve Dallas is almost relieved. The clues point towards ritual murder, but Eve knows there is nothing supernatural about a deadly lust for power . . .

Missing in Death: Aboard the Staten Island ferry, a tourist sees something she shouldn't have — and soon no one can find her. But if she didn't jump, and she's not on board, where is she? Lieutenant Eve Dallas and her team know that all the answers lie in just what was seen on that ferry . . .